"You're a witnes... witness.

"You are the witness who is going to break this case for me. The witness who's going to get me my old job back. Now—do you understand what I want from you?"

She nodded. Her body had gone cold and still. He must have felt it, because he let go of her arms, exhaled and muttered, "Good…" He bent down to pick up his hat from the mossy creek bank where she'd tossed it.

She cleared her throat. "You want me to testify," she said carefully, feeling nothing at all, except cold. "You want me to say I saw who killed those two feds."

"I'm sorry you've had to go through all this for nothing, but I didn't see *anything*. Do you get it?" She sucked in another breath. "So, you can go home now."

★ ★ ★

Dear Reader,

Recently, events in my life have brought me back to the valley in the southern Sierra Nevada mountains of California where I grew up. So, it is perhaps fitting that as I begin a new chapter in my life, I begin a new series, as well, and that I have chosen the mountains and deserts of my youth and childhood—rich in beauty, history and romance—as its setting.

The new series, which we are calling The Scandals of Sierra Malone, will follow the efforts of reclusive, eccentric billionaire Sam Malone, now well into his tenth decade. Hoping to connect with his only surviving heirs, four granddaughters he's never met, Sam has invited the four to come to his remote California hacienda to claim their inheritance. For each of the four, the summons is a life-changing event, one that will bring them unexpected adventure, even danger—and, of course, romance.

This, the first book in the series, is Rachel's story. I hope you will find it both heartwarming and compelling, and that it will serve to bring you back to June Canyon Ranch again and again, to join us as the saga continues.

To new beginnings…

Kathleen Creighton

KATHLEEN CREIGHTON

Sheriff's Runaway Witness

ROMANTIC

SUSPENSE

Recycling programs
for this product may
not exist in your area.

ISBN-13: 978-0-373-27726-1

SHERIFF'S RUNAWAY WITNESS

Books by Kathleen Creighton

Romantic Suspense

*The Awakening of Dr. Brown #1057
*The Seduction of Goody Two Shoes #1089
Virgin Seduction #1148
*The Black Sheep's Baby #1161
Shooting Star #1232
**The Top Gun's Return #1262
**An Order of Protection #1292
**Undercover Mistress #1340
**Secret Agent Sam #1363
The Sheriff of Heartbreak County #1400
The Rebel King #1432
Lazlo's Last Stand #1492
†Danger Signals #1507
†Daredevil's Run #1523
†Lady Killer #1559
†Kincaid's Dangerous Game #1563
†Memory of Murder #1607
††Sheriff's Runaway Witness #1656

*Into the Heartland
**Starrs of the West
†The Taken
††Scandals of Sierra Malone

KATHLEEN CREIGHTON

has roots deep in the California soil but has relocated to South Carolina. As a child, she enjoyed listening to old-timers' tales, and her fascination with the past only deepened as she grew older. Today, she says she is interested in everything—art, music, gardening, zoology, anthropology and history, but people are at the top of her list. She also has a lifelong passion for writing, and now combines all her loves in romance novels.

For Gail and Patience,
(Who is the personification of her name,)
For forebearance, kindness and understanding
Above and beyond all reasonable expectation.

Prologue

From the memoirs of Sierra Sam Malone:

I never thought I would live so long. For the fact that I have done so I must give credit to the Man Upstairs, I suppose, but also to three beautiful women, all of whom loved me a sight more than I deserved. Lord knows I never did right by any of them, but maybe there is still time before I die to make up for some of the wrong I did. I sure do mean to try.

Telling the story—the whole truth…well, I reckon that's as good a place to start as any.

Part One—Elizabeth

That day outside of Barstow when the railroad bulls beat me senseless and threw me off the train and left me to die in the desert wasn't the first time Death came for me and went away empty-handed. Not the first time, but I thought for sure it was the last, and my last day on earth before I'd even reached the ripe age of eighteen. It would have been, too, if not for a bit of crazy dumb luck...and a sweet bit of a girl named Elizabeth.

I don't recall much of that day, and even if I did I wouldn't bore anybody to death telling about it. I do recollect that it was April, and the desert was blazing hot in the daytime and freezing cold when the sun went down. I know I walked when I could and crawled when I couldn't walk anymore, and tried to take shelter in the heat of the day underneath any kind of bush big enough to offer a morsel of shade. I know I got more prickles than comfort from that effort, and that I was plain fool lucky I didn't try to share some rattlesnake's midday napping place.

For some reason—instinct, I reckon, or Divine Guidance, or maybe it was just because, being a mountain boy born and bred from the green hills of West Virginia, and I had no wish to die in the desert—I didn't try to follow the tracks back to Barstow but instead kept stumbling my dogged way toward the mountains I could see off in the distance. Could just as well have been a mirage, but it wasn't. It was mountains, real ones, and something in me told me there might be water there, somewhere.

Well...if there was water in those barren hills it eluded me, and I knew the sands in my hourglass were fast running out. I won't die like a dog on my belly in the dirt, I told myself, and with my last ounce of strength, rose to my feet to shake my fist at the heavens and that terrible killing sun. And as if to punish me for my defiance, at that moment the earth fell out from under my feet, and down, down I fell, rolling and tumbling in a torrent of rock and sand...down, down until I fetched up finally in the bottom of a gully, skinned up and bloodier than the railroad bulls had left me.

Once I'd shaken the cobwebs out of my head and the sand out of my whiskers, I saw something in the side of that gully that nature hadn't put there: a hole, it was. A hole big as *a man is tall. A hole dug by men. And in that part of the country, there was only one thing it could be, and that was a mine.*

Now, as I said, I'm from the hills of West Virginia, and I know a thing or two about mines. One thing I knew was that a lot of the time there's water to be found in those mines, water that can take life as well as give it.

Well, I didn't hesitate. I scrambled up the side of that gully like a madman, clawing my way with bleeding hands. When I got inside the cave and the blessed shade enveloped me, I could smell it. I'd heard tell of animals—horses and cattle and such—being able to smell it, though I'd never thought it had much of a smell, myself. But in that moment I knew it did.

Water.

Yes, sir, I could smell water somewhere in that mine tunnel, and I stumbled my way toward it like a crippled moth fluttering its feeble way to the flame. Deeper and deeper into that tunnel I went, until it was too dark to see my hand in front of my face. I felt my way along the walls, and when my feet got wet I fell to my knees, then flat on my face in that blessed pool. An underground spring, it was, and it had flooded that mine, as water has a way of doing, often to the woe of the miners unlucky enough to get trapped by it. But that day it saved one poor soul, and that was yours truly, Sam Malone.

I drank my fill and then must have passed out for a spell, and when I opened my eyes next I thought I'd died after all. There was light where there shouldn't have been, a soft, golden glow, and I recall thinking, Lord, I don't know how or why but I made it to Heaven! Because where that light hit the water and the walls of that mine tunnel, it gave back a sparkle, a shine I'd only heard about in the stories men told around the fires in the hobo camps alongside the railroad tracks. I understood, then, the madness that drove men to leave everything they knew and the kinfolk that loved them, throw it all away to follow the lure of the gold.

Could it be? In awe, almost in a trance, I dipped my hand into the pool of water and held it up to my face and stared at the flecks that stuck to my skin. Yep, no doubt about it—it was gold.

Before my brain could get to understanding what had happened to me, before I could think what kind of miracle I'd stumbled across, the light moved and sent my shadow dancing long and crooked across the tunnel wall. And a voice spoke to me from the blackness behind the light.

"You're trespassing."

That is how I found my first treasure. Her name was Elizabeth.

She had the face of an angel, but any notions I might have had about being in Heaven went flying straight out of my head when I saw, by the light of the lantern in her hand, the shotgun she carried cradled in one arm and leveled straight and true at my heart.

Chapter 1

Mojave Desert, California
Present day

Jethro Jefferson Fox the Third—or J.J., as he was more commonly known—was in a surly mood. This, despite the fact that the weather was predicted to be sunny and the temperature to top out at around a balmy seventy-five degrees. And, after the past week's rain, there were still lingering patches of green on the hillsides and even some flowers hanging on, which he happened to know was about as good as it got in the Mojave Desert of Southern California.

However, having grown up in the verdant hills of North Carolina, J.J. was pining for—no, *grieving* for—*green*. All the sweet soft shades of green, of roadsides and cow pastures emerging from the dead brown of winter, of new-leafed hardwood trees and deep dark piney woods and underneath in the developing shade, the snowy white of dogwood blooms and lavender-pink of redbuds.

Helluva place for the son of southern Appalachian moonshiners to wind up, he thought, where the green happened in the middle of winter and if you blinked you missed it, and the nearest thing to shade came from spiky clumps of Joshua trees.

The image glaring back at him from the half-silvered mirror over the wash basin in his cramped trailer-sized bathroom gave him no joy, either: hair sun-bleached and crawling well past his collar; facial hair grown beyond the fashionable stubble look and rapidly approaching Grizzly Adams; blue eyes developing a permanent squint in spite of the aviator shades he nearly always wore. The hair and beard had probably originally been some sort of rebellion against his exile to this hellhole, but as it turned out, nobody in the department seemed to give a damn what he looked like, and with the springtime about to turn into summer it was too damn hot anyhow. Time for the shrubbery to go.

He picked up a razor and was contemplating where best to begin mowing, when his radio squawked at him from the bedside table where it spent most nights—those he wasn't out and about on San Bernardino County Sheriff's Department business. He picked it up, thumbed it on and muttered a go-ahead to Katie Mendoza, on morning duty at the station desk.

First, he heard a nervous chuckle. Then: "I wasn't sure I should call you with this, Sheriff."

"Well, you did," J.J. said, returning the baleful stare of the dog sprawled across the foot of his unmade bed, head now raised and ears pricked, awaiting developments. "Might as well tell me."

"I thought it was a joke, first call I got. Then 911 dispatch got one. So I figured I better—"

"Spit it out." J.J. was thinking, *Not much chance it's a dead body, not with a lead-in like that.* He didn't feel too much guilt at the fact that such a thought would cross his mind, either. He could only hope...

"You're not gonna believe it," Katie said with another nervous laugh.

"Try me," said J.J., trying not to grind his teeth.

"Well, okay." Some throat clearing came across the airwaves, followed by a semi-professional-sounding monotone. "Sheriff, we've received several reports of a person walking through the desert, out in the middle of nowhere, an undetermined distance from the highway, off Death Valley Road. No sign of a vehicle anywhere in the vicinity."

"Uh-huh." J.J. waited, figuring there had to be more.

After another episode of throat-clearing, it came. "J.J., swear to God, I am not making this up. This person—it—she—appears to be a *nun*."

Beverly Hills, California
Approximately twelve hours earlier

"He's going to kill me."

Even as she said it Rachel thought, *People say that all the time. My mom, dad, boyfriend, husband...so-and-so is going to kill me. It's just a saying. It doesn't mean anything.*

Rachel meant it. Now she waited to see if she would be believed. She closed her bedroom door and leaned against it, breath held, waiting. Hoping.

"I'm sure he plans to," Sister Mary Isabelle stated matter-of-factly, drawing back to examine the bruises on Rachel's cheek and jaw. Her brown eyes narrowed but she didn't comment. She crossed the room and seated herself on the bed, carefully arranging the folds of her habit around her. "You know too much. And—" she nodded in the direction of Rachel's bulging belly "—once your baby's born, Carlos won't need you any longer."

Rachel let out her breath in a gust and realized she was dangerously close to tears. To be believed was an almost overwhelming relief. She gazed at her oldest and dearest friend in affectionate awe and took refuge in laughter. "Izzy, sometimes I can't believe you're a nun. You're way more worldly than I am."

Sister Mary Isabelle gave an un-nunlike snort. "I'm sure I am—although technically, you know, I'm a 'sister,' not a nun. Why wouldn't I be? Here in the Delacortes' family enclave you're more cloistered than I have ever been. Plus, I'm a doctor, dear heart. My clinic is located in a part of the city that sees more of the bad stuff of life than you ever will—gang violence, drugs, domestic abuse, teen pregnancy. A habit doesn't shelter me from all that, you know."

"Yes, and speaking of that," Rachel said, as the fact registered belatedly, "why are you? I don't think I've ever seen you wear one before."

Sister Mary Isabelle smiled, making her cheeks look like round pink apples within the confines of the wimple. "I have my reasons, which will become clear shortly." She took Rachel's hands in both of hers and squeezed them. "I've been worried about you, you know. I thought you were making a huge mistake when you left in the middle of your first year of internship to marry—"

"And you've told me so," Rachel said dryly. "More than once."

Sister Mary Isabelle was silent for a moment. Then she touched Rachel's bruised cheek—a feather's touch, but still Rachel jerked away from it as if from a slap. "Did Carlos do this?"

"Of course he did—and I know what you're thinking," Rachel said angrily. "Nicky would never have hit me. Never. He wasn't like that. He was nothing like Carlos."

"Chelly...Nicholas was Carlos's son. He grew up with a father who hits women. You *know* the odds are—"

"Nicky was *nothing* like his father." Rachel repeated it as she had so many times in her mind. Willing herself to believe it. She *had* believed it. Until...

"You were in love," Sister Mary Isabelle said sadly, "and you wanted to believe he would have been able to break away from his father's organization. From his influence. Maybe he could have—only God knows. The fact that he was killed before he had the chance to try is tragic. But," she added sternly, "the fact that two federal law enforcement officers were also killed in that shootout is even more tragic." She paused to give Rachel a penetrating stare. "You know that, don't you?"

Rachel nodded silently. She'd been living with that knowledge, that guilt, for months.

"The fact that you happened to be pregnant when Nicholas died bought you some time," Sister Mary Isabelle went on, her voice grave. "But you must know Carlos Delacorte will never trust your loyalty. And—" her eyes twinkled with humor "—he's never really liked you, anyway, has he?"

Rachel managed a wry smile in response. "What's not to like? A nice girl from a Catholic school, on her way to becoming a doctor—"

"—with a moral compass, a *conscience*..."

Rachel sighed. "Well, yes, there is that. Carlos does hate me. And I think he actually blames me for Nicky's death."

Sister Mary Isabelle gave another snort. "He can't live with his own share of fault in getting his son killed, so he needs someone else to dump it on."

Unable to sit still, Rachel began to pace, steps jerky and uneven, one hand on her tight belly. "I'm sure he sees this baby as his second chance. It's Nicky's child. His own flesh and blood. Carlos can't wait to get his hands on it." She suddenly had to hold on to the edge of the tall dresser as fear weakened her knees. "Izzy," she whispered, "I think he plans to take my baby away from me the moment he's born. That's probably when he'll do it, you know—kill me. While I'm out of it—helpless. He'll figure out a way to make it seem like complications of delivery, or something. Not that he'd do it himself, of course—he'd probably let Georg or Stan have the privilege of smothering me with a pillow. They'd enjoy—"

She was enveloped in the crisp folds of Sister Mary Isabelle's habit. It smelled of soap and starch, and an arm was firm and strong around her middle.

Through the rushing sound in her ears she heard Sister Mary Isabelle's voice, calm and firm—her physician's voice. "Hush. That's not going to happen. And right now you are going to stop this drama. The last thing you or your baby needs is for you to panic."

Knowing she was right didn't help much. "I don't know what I'm going to do," Rachel whispered as she allowed herself to be settled on the edge of the bed. "They watch me every second, Izzy. I feel so…trapped. It's gotten much worse since I got the letter…."

Sister Mary Isabelle straightened, instantly alert. "What letter?"

Rachel wiped her eyes. "It came two days ago. By special courier—I had to sign for it personally, with my I.D. Carlos wasn't here, otherwise I doubt I would ever have gotten it. Even then, Carlos's watchdogs wanted to take it away from me, but I opened it and read it with the courier standing right there. There wasn't much they could do about it, short of killing both of us on the spot." She paused to gulp back a laugh she was aware could easily spiral into hysteria. "I'm sure they would have enjoyed that, too, but it would have been a little hard to cover up."

"The letter?" Sister Mary Isabelle prompted.

Rachel caught a quick, shallow breath; these days deeper ones were becoming harder to manage. "Yes. It was from— you're not going to believe this, Izzy—my grandfather."

"Your—oh, you mean the eccentric billionaire? The one who—"

"—abandoned my grandmother and didn't even come to the memorial service when my dad—his own son—was killed? And never once tried to get in touch with me after Grandmother found me in that Manila orphanage and went through all kinds of hell to bring me to America? Yeah, *that* grandfather. *Sam Malone.* He wrote to me, can you believe it?"

"What on earth did he want?" Sister Mary Isabelle's eyes were shining now with interest. "I didn't know he was still alive. He must be…how old?"

"*Very* old. I'm not sure exactly, but in his nineties, I think. Maybe even a hundred. I don't know what he wants, to tell you the truth. Something about an inheritance—which I certainly don't want. Seriously. I don't want a thing from that man." Rachel curved her hand over her lower abdomen and the envelope affixed there with surgical tape gave a faint crackle. She felt the baby roil as if in response. Her brief flare of anger had already faded, leaving her once more feeling frightened and vulnerable.

So, she'd managed to protect the letter, big deal. Now what? She'd never felt so helpless.

She took another shallow breath. "I don't want anything from Sam Malone—not for me. But maybe it's—you know… the fact that it came just now, when I've been wondering how in the world I can get away from here…I've been thinking, maybe it's not a coincidence."

"I don't believe in coincidence. Sometimes God works in mysterious ways," Sister Mary Isabelle said serenely. Then, with her customary practicality: "What did you do with the letter? Did Carlos take it?"

Rachel shook her head and smiled a fierce, defiant smile. "It's here," she whispered, rubbing her belly. "The letter. I taped it to my stomach." Sister Mary Isabelle gave a whoop of laughter, and Rachel gulped down a giggle. "Yes, and when Carlos demanded that I turn it over to him, I told him I'd hidden it where he'd never find it." She sniffed. "Not even Carlos would dare to violate me *there*."

"Clever girl. Good for you." Sister Mary Isabelle immediately grew somber again. Her always expressive eyes darkened with sorrow as she lifted one hand and cupped Rachel's bruised cheek. "But he did lay a hand on you. Was that when he hit you?"

Rachel nodded, remembering pain and outrage. And fury. "When I told him I'd hidden the letter where he'd never find it. It was out of sheer frustration, I think." Her lips tightened bitterly. "He's been so careful up till now."

Sister Mary Isabelle suddenly leaned closer to whisper in her ear. "Are there surveillance cameras in this room?"

The question didn't surprise Rachel; it was one she'd asked herself often enough. She shook her head and whispered back, "I don't think so. I've looked."

"What about bugs?"

She gave a humorless laugh. "I don't know why Carlos would bother with bugs when I don't have access to phone, internet or, with the exception of yourself, visitors. But when I want to be sure of at least some privacy..." She took two steps toward the door and reached for the light switch. "There," she whispered as the room was plunged into darkness. She punched a button on the clock radio on her bedside table and a Bruce Springsteen song filled the silence. "Now, what did you want to tell me?"

"Good for you." Sister Mary Isabelle's chuckle came from

the shadows. "I've come to spring you. It's time you got yourself and that baby of yours out of this *Hell* you're in—and being Roman Catholic, I do not use that term lightly."

At the first words, Rachel had smothered an involuntary cry with her fingertips. Now her gaze jerked to the windows, where, as the room behind her darkened, the panorama of the lights of Los Angeles had come into view. The world out there…how many times had she gazed at that incredible vista, stretching from the mountains to the sea, and felt like an animal in a cage. Trapped.

"How?" she whispered. "Can you work miracles?"

"I'm a sister, not a saint." Izzy sounded amused.

In the near darkness, the deeper shadow that was Sister Mary Isabelle moved and rustled mysteriously. Rachel waited in suspense, breath held. Then warm hands clutched her cold ones, and something—a bundle of fabric that smelled of soap and starch—was thrust into her arms.

"What—"

"Shush—I told you I'd explain the habit. It's for you, of course. I'm wearing my regular clothes underneath. Here," she added, when Rachel stood motionless, stunned, "I'll help you put it on."

Sister Mary Isabelle explained in a whisper as her hands turned and tugged Rachel this way and that. "Leave your own clothes on, of course. So you can ditch the habit as soon as you're safely away from the compound. Good thing I'm… shall we say, generously built, hmm? You'd be way too tiny and this would be a tent on you under normal circumstances, but with that nine-month baby bump, plus the clothes you're wearing—there, how does that feel?"

"Izzy, I—"

"Oops—hold still—these wimples are a bit tricky… Okay. I think that's got it. Now listen carefully. You're going to have to keep your head down, okay? I doubt anybody is going to look past the habit, anyway, but just to be on the safe side. Take my car—it's out there in the driveway beside the fountain—the white Toyota. The keys are in it. Oh, and I—ahem—took the liberty of borrowing the plates from Father Francis's secretary's car. She took the train down to San Diego for a conference and won't be needing them for a few days. I really hope she doesn't mind contributing to the cause...." Having finished adjusting the disguise to her liking, she took Rachel firmly by the arms and gave her a small shake. "Now. Listen carefully, dear. You'll need to stop as soon as you're safely away and put the right plates back on—they're in the trunk—so you don't get stopped for having the wrong ones, okay?"

A dozen questions surged through Rachel's mind. She managed to verbalize the most urgent. "But Izzy, what about you? How will you—I can't think what Carlos will do when he—"

Strong hands gripped hers. "Nothing is going to happen to me. Carlos may be a ruthless criminal, a mob boss, but he's also a devout Catholic—even he won't dare to harm a nun. Or sister." Rachel could hear the smile in her voice. "I intend to stay right here in the dark for as long as it takes someone to get suspicious and come to check on you. The longer the better, obviously, so you'll get a good head start. If all goes well, you should be able to disappear before anyone here knows you're gone. Then, you can look up that grandfather of yours. If you want to, of course. If he can't protect you, maybe he can at least provide you with the money to start a new life somewhere, with a new identity."

"My own private witness protection program," Rachel said on a small note of sobbing laughter. "Izzy, I don't know what to say. How can I ever thank you?"

"Thank me by having and raising a happy, healthy baby, somewhere away from all this violence and danger, that's how.

And do *not* try to get in touch with me, understand? Who knows what resources Carlos Delacorte has at his disposal. Now go, before—oh, wait. Forgot the most important thing." There was a faint whisper of sound, and Sister Mary Isabelle placed something in Rachel's hands. She closed Rachel's hands around the object, folded within her own.

"Your rosary," Rachel whispered. "Izzy, I can't. Really." She gave a nervous laugh. "Besides, I don't think I've prayed since high school."

"Keep it anyway," Sister Mary Isabelle said firmly. "You never know when the mood might strike you. And just because you've forgotten how to pray doesn't mean God's forgotten how to listen. Speaking of which…" There was a moment of silence, followed by a whispered, "Amen…" and the familiar little flurry of movement that was Sister Mary Isabelle crossing herself. Then the strong, capable hands—physician's hands—took hers once more.

"Now—remember. No driver's license, no identification, no credit cards. Right? Do you have any money? Cash?" Rachel shook her head. "Well, never mind—I left some for you in the car. Not much, but it should get you to your grandfather. No cell phone—oh, that's right, you don't have one. Just as well. If television cop shows are right, they could probably track you that way. So—have I forgotten anything?"

"I can't imagine what," Rachel said with a laugh, and added in a shaky whisper, "Izzy, what if I—"

"You're going to be fine." The fabric of the habit rustled as Sister Mary Isabelle pulled her close in a quick, hard hug. "Now go." And after a pause, she added a fervent, *"Vaya con Dios."*

Go with God. If only I believed that, Rachel thought.

The reality was, it was all up to her now. Izzy had given her the chance she needed, but finally, *she* would have to do what was necessary to save herself and her baby.

She took one last breath, the deepest she could manage, and whispered, "'Bye, Izzy. Thank you." Then she opened the door and slipped into the hallway.

After the darkness, the indirect lighting in the hallway, subdued as it was, struck her like a spotlight; she almost expected to hear sirens blaring and steel doors clanging shut. Her heart thumped so hard it hurt her chest as she hurried toward the stairs. Remembering to keep her face lowered, she took courage from the knowledge that it would be shielded from the watchful eyes of the security cameras by the starched wings of the wimple.

A hard grip on the banister didn't entirely prevent her hand from shaking, and she found herself clutching the rosary in her other hand, thrust deep in the folds of the habit. She'd meant what she'd told Izzy, about not knowing any longer how to pray, and in fact she didn't know if she even believed in such things now. But somehow, as the rosary beads pressed hard into her flesh, she felt a sense of purpose come over her. Purpose, resolve, strength—a surge of power that seemed to rise from some place deep within her. Maternal instinct of some sort, probably. The absolute certainty that she would do whatever it took to protect the tiny life nestled beneath her heart.

A life that was becoming increasingly impatient with its confinement, it seemed. Halfway down the curving staircase she had to pause for a moment to wait for the steel band that had tightened around her belly to relax. Braxton Hicks contractions, she told herself. Although this was the strongest she'd felt yet, she knew they were still nothing to worry about.

The tightening eased, and she continued down the stairs, head bowed. The security guards in the cavernous entry gave her a lazy glance when she stepped onto the quarry tile floor. Their eyes were flat and expressionless, although they both nodded with a modicum of respect—the habit, again. As she swept past them, habit swishing over the baked adobe, one of the guards even stepped ahead of her to open the heavy, ornately carved doors. Then he stood and watched her descend the steps at the slow and stately pace befitting a nun in full habit—or a woman in her ninth month of pregnancy. Rachel could feel those hard, cold eyes on her as she crossed the brick-paved courtyard, but her newfound courage kept her from giving in to the urge to look back or hurry her steps.

She found that she felt both shielded and bolstered by the voluminous folds of the habit, as if it was a suit of armor rather than mere cloth. The wimple that hid her face from the eagle eyes of the security guards and cameras also kept her focused, her own eyes firmly concentrated on her immediate goal: *Walk to the car...don't hurry...open the door...ease in behind the wheel...not too tight a fit, thank God Izzy's bigger than I am...keys in ignition...turn on...put car in gear...drive away...don't hurry...don't hurry...slowly...slowly.*

The big iron gates slid open as she approached...then silently closed behind her. At the bottom of the drive she paused, left-turn blinker off-sync with the frantic rhythm of her pounding heart. She made the turn and rolled slowly down the curving street, every part of her wanting to step on the accelerator and screech away at all possible speed. But she forced herself to go slowly...slowly. She rounded the first bend, and the red tile roofs of the Delacorte compound were now hidden from her view. She let out her breath in a gust, and wondered how long she'd been holding it.

For the moment, yes, she was free. But she had a long way to go before she—and her baby—would be safe.

Her game plan was simple. She would head east on the interstate as fast as traffic and the law allowed, and go as far as roughly half of the almost-full tank of gas in Izzy's car would take her. After that, she would get off the main roads, buy herself some food and as much gasoline as the money Izzy had left her would buy, and cut back north and west across the desert to the remote southern Sierra Valley where her grandfather's ranch was. She would avoid places with people, so as to leave as few witnesses as possible. She would not risk going to the police or any other public agency for help; she didn't know how far the Delacorte family's influence might reach. Best to stay anonymous. Play it safe. *Trust no one.*

Before getting on the freeway, though, mindful of Izzy's instructions, she drove to a shopping center she remembered from the days when she was free to come and go as she pleased, and drove into the center's underground parking structure. She found a remote and relatively unused level and parked in the shadow of a support pillar. She took off the habit—with regret; she'd liked the feeling of safety it had given her—and put it in the trunk of the car. It had occurred to her that leaving it might serve as a marker, a signpost for those who might be trying to track her down, like a footprint or a broken twig. Better to leave no traces of herself behind.

She found the license plates Izzy had left in the trunk, along with a screwdriver, and was pleased to note as she took the borrowed plates off and put the correct ones on that her hands didn't shake. She no longer felt terrified. Keyed up, excited, euphoric almost, but not afraid. That alone was a wonderful and amazing thing. She'd been afraid for so long.

Back on the freeway, which was moving relatively swiftly at that time of evening, she opened her window, shook her hair free of the elastic band that had held it back from her face and reveled in the sensation of the cool spring wind lifting strands off her shoulders, tickling her ears and temples.

This is what freedom feels like.

But then a pair of headlights came zooming up behind her and, as her heart leaped into her throat, whipped impatiently around her on the left and sped away in the fast lane. After that, heart hammering, she kept checking her rearview mirrors even though the anonymous headlights she saw reflected there had nothing to tell her.

Just past the Ontario Airport she turned off onto Interstate 15, heading northeast toward Las Vegas. Several times already the almost constant pressure on her bladder had forced her off the freeway in search of a public restroom, and during one of these pit stops she had bought a map. She had studied it while munching cheese-flavored popcorn and bottled water from the rest stop's vending machines, and had plotted what she thought seemed like the best route—meaning the most devious, the least likely. Just past the town of Barstow where I-15 intersected with I-40 she had discovered a numbered highway that seemed to run in a reasonably straight line northward to Death Valley. Perfect, she thought. Who would ever think to look for her in Death Valley?

Having settled on her travel route, Rachel still had decisions to make. Looking at the map, the road she'd chosen, though a numbered state route and therefore probably fairly well maintained, seemed lonely and remote, and she wasn't quite brave enough—or stupid enough—to chance it alone at night. Neither would she feel safe in a motel anywhere in a major crossroads like Barstow, which would be the obvious place for Carlos to look for her. Even a maintained rest stop seemed too exposed, too risky.

Maybe she was being overly paranoid, but she'd learned a lot about the Delacorte family in the two years she'd been a part of it, and she wouldn't make the mistake of underestimating its resources. Not when her life and the future of her unborn child depended on it.

So, after making one last bathroom stop and replenishing her supply of snacks and drinking water, she pulled off onto a minor paved road leading into the desert. The pavement fizzled out after only a quarter of a mile or so, but since she could no longer see the lights of traffic on the interstate, she felt it would be a reasonably safe place to spend what was left of the night. Not that she expected to sleep; the night was chilly, the baby was restless and her back ached. But she crawled into the backseat anyway, and curled up on her side with her head pillowed on one folded arm, the other hand resting on her swollen belly. She closed her eyes, and within minutes, as they so often did, images of Nicky came to fill the blank screen of her mind.

Happy images, at first—memories of when they'd first met, on the grounds of UCLA. She'd been premed, and Nicky—well, who knew what his major was? Undeclared, probably, but he'd been taking a few classes she'd shared, just to see, he'd told her, if medicine held any interest for him. She remembered his smile, the sparkle of mischief in his beautiful dark eyes. She'd led a protected life up to that point, and the aura of danger that seemed to surround him had been…exciting.

His face filled her mind now, and she braced for the pain. Pushed against it, like worrying a sore tooth with her tongue. The memory came less easily now, six months after his death, and she felt a brief surge of panic when she couldn't seem to find it at first. Then it swept over her and she pressed her hand against the spot in the middle of her chest where the pain was sharpest. Pressed against it and gasped in sharp breaths, fighting it back. She both welcomed and dreaded the pain, knowing that when the day came she could no longer summon it, Nicky would be truly, finally gone.

But for now…the pain seemed familiar, almost comforting. She let it settle over her and the tears ooze from beneath her lashes and trickle in cool trails down the side of her face and into her hair while memories, images played through her head. Happy memories, these were…the two of them together at the beach, on the sailboat in Newport, skiing in Park City, riding down Pacific Coast Highway in Nicky's Porsche with the top down and the wind blowing through her hair. Laughing. Making love in all sorts of places, Nicky smiling down into her eyes while their bodies moved together in lovely harmony. Telling him she was pregnant, hearing the delighted whoop of his laughter, watching his eyes dance with almost childlike joy.

Then…they were dancing together, swaying to the music of old-fashioned bands, holding hands across a table lit by candlelight, and Nicky was placing the ring on her finger. Now…their wedding day, a blur of people and flowers and champagne, and Nicky's family—Carlos had scared her a little even then, but Nicky had told her they wouldn't have to be a part of the Delacorte organization, they would have their own lives, raise their children the way they wanted to.

And she had believed him then.

More music…more dancing…but the mood had darkened. She didn't know what it was, but something was wrong. Nicky was different. She didn't know why, but she felt…afraid.

We're dancing, Nicky and I…and suddenly we're not dancing, but running, running, and Nicky has hold of my hand and I'm running as fast as I can trying to keep up with him. Somehow we're not in a ballroom anymore, but in an alley, and Nicky pushes me down behind a trash bin. I hear the roar of car engines, the chirp of sirens and then the world explodes in gunfire. Funny—I've never heard gunfire before, but I know instantly what it is. Nicky calls out to me, calls my name. I look over at him and I see blood. It's everywhere, on his clothes and on my hands. His eyes are open, looking at me, and they aren't sparkling, laughing, gleaming with mischief. They look so frightened. Terrified. And then…there is nothing.

Someone grabs me, pulls me, half carries me, pushes

me into a car and everything is chaos. But I remember the guns, and the smell of blood and gasoline and smoke, and I remember the bodies lying in the wet and dirt of the alley. I remember...I remember.

Chapter 2

She woke up, struggled to sit up in the cramped confines of the car. Her heart was hammering, her body stiff and aching in the early morning chill. For a moment she was unable to grasp where she was. The light outside the car windows was the cold gray light of dawn, not the glaring, pulsing hellish kaleidoscope of colors, of nighttime and police lights and spotlights. The vista beyond the windows was barren, empty, a landscape of pastels dotted with dark splotches and freckles of lava rock, not a canyon of steel and concrete and oily black pavement glistening with rain and blood.

The only thing left from her nightmare was the fear. The sense of danger and doom.

The baby stirred beneath her ribs. And she remembered.

Izzy. Izzy came in her habit. This is Izzy's car. I'm driving Izzy's car, and I'm free of the Delacortes at last. Free!

Yes, she was free, but alone out in the middle of nowhere. She still had to get to someone who could help her, someone she could trust. She had to find a safe place, which meant a place where Carlos would never find her. *If there is such a place*.

She ran her hand under her belly, and the letter she'd taped there crackled faintly. *Sam Malone's letter*. Would the grandfather she'd never known, the grandfather who had never acknowledged her or lifted a finger or spent a dime to help her or her grandmother, would such a man be able to help her now? Was he even alive? If he was, as distasteful as it was to her to have to ask for help, it seemed her only choice. She would go to the place, this place called June Canyon Ranch, and after that…well, she would have to wait and see.

Meanwhile, the pressure on her bladder was intense, and she was a long way from any public restroom. She climbed stiffly out of the car and relieved herself, as awkward and embarrassing as that process was, then stretched her legs by walking gingerly around the car several times. Her back ached terribly, but she supposed that was to be expected after spending a night in the backseat of a Toyota, nine months pregnant.

After a breakfast of bottled water and a package of bite-sized chocolate chip cookies that did little to calm her hunger pangs, Rachel consulted her map once more, then eased herself behind the wheel. She started up the car, managed to get it turned around without getting stuck in the soft sand and headed back to the interstate. Backtracking toward Barstow, she found the exit she wanted, the one for the numbered state route that ran north toward Death Valley. Exhilaration filled her as she made the turn, and saw the ribbon of asphalt stretching out into the lava-rock-studded hills. As the sun rose she saw that the hills weren't barren at all, but tinged a lovely shade of green and splashed here and there with the vibrant yellows and purples and oranges of desert spring wildflowers.

Oh, but it felt good, so good to be free.

She drove fast—maybe too fast—and met a few cars at first, probably coming from one of the tiny dots she'd seen on the map, settlements too small to be called towns. At this hour they'd be heading into Barstow to school or work, she guessed. Then the sun rose and there were fewer cars. The miles sped by and the mountains seemed no closer. She hadn't expected such distances between signs of civilization.

Though the desert seemed endless, it wasn't empty and parched as she'd expected. The landscape alternated between plains where wildflowers made a solid yellow carpet between clumps of sagebrush and those greenish rock-strew hills. The road ran straight across the plains and wound through some hills, then seemed to follow a dry wash, or ravine. There were no other cars now. Rachel was alone, just her and the empty ribbon of highway stretching out to where the pale blue sky met the pastel-colored earth.

She hadn't expected it to be so beautiful. There—was that a patch of poppies blooming over on the hillside?

She glanced back at the road ahead—which suddenly wasn't empty anymore. Incredibly, there was a dog—or, good Lord, could it be a *coyote?*—smack in the middle of the road. Trotting down the road as if he had the right-of-way—which, Rachel supposed, he did, really.

She had already jerked the wheel to the right, reflexively. Now, realizing she was about to drive into the sand and sagebrush, she overcorrected to the left. The next thing she knew, the little Toyota was careening wildly through the brush and cactus, and she was hanging on to the steering wheel, frozen in fear.

The brake! Step on the brake!

She did, but too late. The Toyota had enough momentum to continue up an embankment before toppling slowly down… down…to rest with a crunch, nose-first in the soft sand at the bottom of the dry wash.

For a few moments Rachel sat absolutely still. Stunned. Then the first coherent thought came: *My baby!*

Terrified, she held her breath and took stock. *Okay. Nothing hurts. Besides my back, anyway.*

Nothing seemed amiss. In fact, thanks to that last-minute stomp on the brake pedal, she'd evidently landed in the wash with so little impact the air bag hadn't even deployed. And her seat belt had kept her belly from hitting the steering wheel. Still, she was pressed up against it. Which couldn't be good.

She opened the door—which required little effort, thanks to the angle of the car—released the seat belt and half slid, half fell onto the steeply sloping bank of the ravine. She pulled up her feet and sat there braced and hugging herself, waiting until she felt her legs were steady enough to hold her.

Stupid. How could I have been so careless? Stupid, stupid! What now?

She'd never be able to get the car out of the ravine without a tow truck. But of course she had no cell phone, no way to call for help. Hopefully, a car would come along, but then… what if… In her vulnerable state, the paranoia of the night before returned.

Oh, God, what if Carlos is out looking for me? What if he's somehow managed to track me here?

No, she didn't dare flag down a passing stranger. She had to get to some sort of settlement—one of those tiny dots on the map. Surely there would be someone there with a telephone. She could walk—it couldn't be that far. She'd been driving for what seemed like forever. She had to have already covered most of the distance to the next one.

Holding on to the open door, she pulled herself to her feet. Though it was a tight squeeze, she managed to stretch across the seat and retrieve the map and what remained of her water and snacks from where they'd slid onto the floor during her wild ride and final descent into the ravine.

So far, so good. But now she became aware of the sun beating down on her unprotected head, and any idiot knew about the dangers of walking in the desert without proper protection.

Then she remembered the habit. Izzy's habit, that she'd tossed so casually into the trunk after she'd made her escape from the Delacorte estate. It would be rather like the robes desert Arabs wore, wouldn't it? *Perfect.*

She pulled the trunk release—gratified to discover it still worked—then managed make her way back up the dirt bank, pulling herself along the side of the car, until she could reach the trunk. She lifted the trunk lid and gathered up the pile of fabric that was Izzy's habit, then had to bend over with it clutched to her chest as pain unlike anything she'd ever known before gripped her back and pelvis like a giant vise.

For a moment she bore it in stoic silence, before she remembered there was no one to hear her, so what did it matter. She let out a primal roar that surprised her almost as much as the fact that it actually seemed to help.

There. It's going away now. Yes. Thank God.

But then, as the pain diminished panic rushed in to take its place.

Oh, my God. That was a contraction. A real one. Not Braxton Hicks. Oh, my God. I'm in labor.

First order of business: Rachel, do not panic!

She leaned against the back of the car and took deep breaths to calm herself. She'd had enough medical training to know that, for the moment, at least, she was in no real danger. This was her first baby. Labor could, and probably would, go on for hours and hours. Plenty of time. Her original plan—to walk to the nearest site of human habitation—would still appear to be the best option. And if she kept reasonably close to the road, she could still flag down someone if it came to that.

If worse came to worst. If she absolutely had to take the chance.

But she wasn't there yet. So far, just that one contraction, and as long as the contractions stayed far apart she'd be okay. No need to panic. She had water, and protection from the sun. She'd be fine.

Determinedly putting all the terrible thoughts and possibilities out of her mind, Rachel stood on the edge of the wash, gazing at the endless panorama of desert and mountains stretching away to cloudless blue skies. *My God,* she thought, *I truly am alone. Utterly and completely alone!*

As if in contradiction of the thought, a little breeze came skirling along through the brush and picked up the wings of her long black hair, tugging it gently at first, then with more urgency. *Hurry up!* it seemed to say. *Come along, you're wasting time!*

Oddly enough, the knowledge that she was indeed on her own, and completely dependent on her own devices, made her feel stronger. She closed her eyes, took a deep breath, opened them again and began to methodically sort out the folds of the habit.

A few minutes later, Rachel set out across the desert, with Izzy's rosary beads clutched in one hand and her last bottle of water in the other.

Sheriff's Deputy J. J. Fox did not take lightly the 911 dispatcher's report of someone walking alone in the desert—nun or otherwise. Fact was, the desert killed people. All the time. Maybe not as often as before cell phones and GPS, but it still happened. Maybe less likely now when the weather was relatively benign as compared to the coming heat of summer, which would be just plain suicidal.

"Some people are too damn stupid to live," he said to his passenger, who was sitting upright on her haunches in the middle of the backseat of the sheriff's department patrol vehicle, drooling on J.J.'s right shoulder. "Too bad we can't just let nature take its course…Darwin's Law, you know? Weed out some of these idiots." Getting only panting sounds in reply, and considerably more dog drool, he gave a gusty sigh. "Yeah…s'pose not. But just between you and me, Moonshine…"

He hoped it was a false alarm, a mirage or…maybe windblown clothing hung up on a cactus. But he had a feeling it wouldn't be; the notion of a woman—a nun!—walking alone in the desert was just nutty enough to be true.

"Really," he said to the drooler, "you couldn't make this stuff up."

As he approached the mile marker the dispatcher had given as the approximate location of the nun sightings, he slowed down and turned on his lights. Crawling along the shoulder at walking speed, he scanned the terrain on both sides of the highway. Nothing he could see, except for the usual scrubby bushes—he was no botanist, so as far as he was concerned they all came under the heading "sagebrush"—now afloat in a sea of golden flowers, with here and there a clump of cholla cacti or Joshua trees to break the monotony. If there had been anybody walking out there, he couldn't see her now, and that wasn't good news.

Swearing to himself, he pulled to a stop on the sandy shoulder. In the backseat, the hound dog of undetermined pedigree licked her chops lustily and wriggled in anticipation while J.J. unhooked his seat belt. He spoke briefly to his shoulder mic, then opened the door of the vehicle and stepped out onto hot white sand. "Okay, Moonshine, how about you and me go and do what they pay us for?"

* * *

Rachel dreamed of Nicholas again. They were together at the beach, a rare hot day in Malibu. She was hot, unpleasantly so. She wanted to get up and run down to the waves to cool off, but for some reason she felt heavy…so heavy she couldn't get up. Then she saw that Nicky was laughing, laughing because he'd buried her up to her neck in the sand. He thought it was all in fun, but she began to be frightened and she begged him to dig her out of the sand and let her up. But he just kept adding more sand, and it was heavy, and the pressure was weighing her down, and then a wave came and splashed her in the face and she woke up, gasping.

Except she thought she must still be dreaming, maybe that twilight dreaming where you are almost awake but not quite enough to make the dreaming stop. Because now, instead of a mountain of sand weighing her down, there was something big and heavy and warm—and *alive!*—sitting on her chest. And instead of cold saltwater bathing her face, it was something slobbery and raspy and odd-smelling. And whatever it was, it was making horrifying snuffling, whimpering sounds.

Terrified, she tried to lift her arms to fend off whatever it was, but found she couldn't move because it was sitting on her arms, too.

"Moonshine! That's enough—come 'ere, girl. What are you trying to do, drown her or smother her?"

Moonshine?

But the slobbery, snuffly, smelly something stopped bathing her face, and the weight lifted abruptly from her chest.

Rachel drew breath in a gasp and opened her eyes. She looked up…and up at a long, tall silhouette against a blue-white sky—but for only an instant, because almost at once the silhouette folded up and came down on one knee beside her in the sandy shade of a clump of Joshua trees. Now she wondered if she could *still* be dreaming, because she found herself gazing at a face that seemed to have come straight out of a Western movie. Steely blue-green eyes stared down at her from the shadows cast by the broad brim of a cowboy hat, eyes that were squinting in apparent concern, causing a fan of lines to radiate from their corners. Sandy blond hair straggled from beneath the hat's brim to feather over a khaki shirt collar, and a thick growth of reddish-brown whiskers failed to hide a mouth that stretched in a thin, unsmiling line.

Once again, she struggled to sit up, but now it was a hand planted firmly on her shoulder that kept her where she was.

"Take it easy, miss…uh, Sister. We're gonna get you some help, okay?" The voice spoke with unmistakable authority. It was deep and scratchy, and matched the weathered and rough-hewn face perfectly. There were traces of an accent, too. Southern, she thought.

The face came closer, bending over her, and fingers touched her face with unexpected gentleness. "Can you tell me who did this to you?" And the voice was at the same time softer and more dangerous. "Are you hurt, uh, anywhere else?"

Two things occurred to Rachel then. One, that she was wearing a nun's habit, which explained her Good Samaritan's reticence—even embarrassment—regarding her person. And two, he'd obviously noticed the bruises on her face.

And following close on the heels of those two realizations came a third: She was probably due for another contraction. Any second.

How was she going to explain *that?*

She pushed at the hand holding her down and managed to prop herself on one elbow. "I'm not hurt," she said, trying not to hold her breath or clench her teeth. Trying to breathe. Normally. Trying not to give away the fact that she hurt *everywhere*. "I was just—I got a little tired, and thirsty and I thought I'd rest a few minutes in the shade. I guess I must have dozed off. I'm okay—really."

The truth was, she'd gotten scared when she'd noticed several cars slowing down as they passed on the highway. That was when she'd hidden behind the grove of spiky Joshua trees. And there'd been a couple of contractions—bad ones—and after that, she'd curled up on her side to rest…just for a minute. She couldn't have been asleep for very long.

The man put his hand under her elbow and helped her to sit up, while at the same time he unhooked a canteen from his belt. He had a lot of other things attached to his belt, she observed as he unscrewed the lid to the canteen and offered it to her. One of which was a gun. And there was a metal star pinned to his shirt. Which she supposed explained a lot of things. And did not reassure her.

Now that he seemed satisfied her circumstances weren't dire, his eyes regarded her more with suspicion than compassion. They narrowed again as he watched her drink. "You want to tell me what you're doing out here in the middle of the desert? Alone?" His voice was a typical lawman's voice: hard and without much expression. "And how you came to have those bruises on your face?"

"Bruises?" The innocent and slightly puzzled frown came easily to her; distrust of law enforcement was automatic now. Awareness of that fact drifted like cloud shadows through her consciousness, along with a sense of sadness and guilt. *I'm sorry, Grandmother. I know you didn't raise me to be like this.*

But the shadows weren't dark enough to stop reflexive responses of caution and cover. "Oh," she said, feigning sudden enlightenment as she wiped water from her lips with the back of her hand. She touched one still-tender cheekbone. "I guess that must have happened when I…"

"When you…" her Good Samaritan prompted when she paused.

Rachel closed her eyes and exhaled. "I feel so stupid. You

see, I swerved to miss a—I guess it must have been a coyote—
well, I'd never seen one, and I was distracted, and the next
thing I knew, I was careening across the desert, and, um, I
wound up in a ditch. Thank God for air bags!" She crossed
herself and cast her gaze prayerfully skyward—a rather nice
touch, she thought, considering what she was wearing.

I wonder if he bought it.

In his long and not always illustrious career as a homicide
detective with the San Bernardino County Sheriff's Department, J. J. Fox had been lied to many times. Although never
before, he was fairly certain, by a nun. He knew what bruises
left by human fists looked like. Plus, now that he'd had a
chance to examine these more closely, he was pretty sure they
were at least a couple of days old.

But who in the hell would beat up a nun?

"When did this happen? This…accident?"

A frown etched delicate pleats between her eyes. Dark
eyes, almost black, so dark he could see himself reflected in
them. Eyes fringed with thick black lashes, and with a slightly
Asian cast, he noted. Probably mixed blood, and if he'd had
to guess, given her size, he'd have said maybe Cambodian or
Vietnamese.

"This morning…I guess it must be afternoon now, right?
I've kind of lost track of time…"

J.J. fingered the radio mic on his shoulder. "We'll get
someone out here to take care of your car, ma'am—uh, Sister.
Can you tell me whereabouts this happened?"

Again the frown. And this time she nibbled delicately on
her lower lip. A very soft and full lower lip, he noted, and
immediately felt ashamed of himself. The woman was a nun,
for God's sake. No disrespect intended.

"Oh—I don't know! I think it was…back that way—no,
wait…I'm so confused. I've been wandering around…maybe

I've been going in circles, do you think so?" Her gaze lifted to his with helpless appeal.

Which might have had more effect on him if he hadn't seen something else in her eyes, something he'd seen all too often, in his line of work, in the eyes of suspects and witnesses alike: a mixture of calculation and fear. This woman really did not trust him. And plainly, she did not want him to find her car. He wondered why.

It didn't bother him too much that she wouldn't give him the location of her vehicle; there had to be evidence of where she'd left the road, which should make it easy enough to locate. But no doubt about it, something about this woman and her situation was off—*way* off. Here was a nun, fairly young— judging from her flawless and unlined skin—of Eurasian ancestry and tiny in stature, out in the middle of the desert, miles from any outposts of civilization, on foot and sporting bruises that had almost certainly come from a beating. Small wonder his cop-radar was pinging like crazy.

He stood up and pivoted away from the woman while he got Katie on his radio and instructed her to send a tow truck out south on Death Valley Road. "Tell Bucky he'll have to hunt for the tire tracks—don't have the exact location, but I'm guessing it's gonna be south of my location a couple miles, at least."

"Got it," Katie said. And after a pause: "So…is she?"

"Is she what?" Although he knew.

"A nun?"

"Remains to be seen," J.J. said, and signed off.

When he turned back to the woman, she was on her hands and knees trying to get up and not being graceful about it. Evidently the lady had gotten herself tangled up in her habit, which seemed to him a little strange. He'd have thought someone used to wearing one of those things would have figured out how to manage it by now. Mentally rolling his eyes, he bent down and got a hand under her elbow and hoisted her to her feet.

No sooner had he done that, than she gave out with a groan, uttered a very un-nunlike word and folded right back up again, while hanging on to his arm with the desperation grip of someone in immediate danger of drowning.

Damn woman might have mentioned she was hurt! Swearing both aloud and mentally, J.J. scooped her up in his arms and hollered for Moonshine, who was panting in the Joshua tree's shade a little way off. He set out with long strides across the sand, and about halfway to his car it occurred to him that, for a little bitty thing, this woman was a whole lot heavier than she looked. Then he looked down at what he was carrying.

What the hell?

What he saw gave him one of the biggest shocks of his life, which was probably why he burst out with the question before he thought how ridiculous it was going to sound. "Sister, are you *pregnant?*"

She didn't even open her eyes. Just went on sort of panting and groaning at the same time, and she had one hand on the huge belly now plainly visible beneath the draping of the habit.

Just holding her against him, he could feel how stiff and seized up she was.

Great. Just great. Not only pregnant, but in labor.

He kept walking, making for his vehicle, until he felt the woman in his arms relax and start breathing somewhat normally again. Then, without slowing his steps, he gritted his teeth and said, "Please tell me you're not really a nun."

She opened one eye and glared up at him. "Is that relevant?"

Relevant? He snorted and walked while he considered that. Probably it wasn't, in her present circumstances. He tried to think whether it bothered him, the thought of a nun being pregnant, and decided against all reason that it did. He couldn't have said why; he wasn't even Catholic, having been raised more or less Baptist, growing up, like most everybody else he'd known back then. But some things were just, well... sacred.

"How far apart are your contractions?" He thought he said it pretty calmly, considering.

"I don't know, I don't have a watch. But I've been counting. I think...about two or three minutes."

J.J. wasn't a doctor, and it had been a long time since those first aid and emergency childbirth classes way back in his training days, but he was pretty sure that wasn't good news. *This just keeps getting better and better,* J.J. thought. He didn't say anything, though, because they'd arrived back at his patrol vehicle, where Moonshine was waiting impatiently for him to open the door, doing a little dance as she tried to keep her feet off the hot sand.

"You're riding shotgun," he said to the dog, and then, without much sympathy, to his burden, "You gonna be okay if I set you down?"

"I'm fine," she said. But he noticed she was looking paler than she ought to, considering the heat and the sheen of sweat he could see on her forehead and the bridge of her nose.

"Okay, then, easy does it..." And he wondered why he couldn't seem to make his voice sound nicer. At least gentler. Sure, he didn't like being lied to, and he wasn't used to being distrusted, at least not by supposedly innocent law-abiding citizens. But this probably wasn't any of her fault; he doubted any woman in her condition would be out here in the middle of the desert by choice. And there were those bruises.

Again with the glare—both eyes, this time. "I'm not made of glass. Just put me down."

So he did. And the minute her feet touched the ground she

sort of gasped and clutched at her belly, then whispered, "Oh, God." It wasn't a prayer.

Moonshine whimpered and moved off a little ways, looking perturbed.

J.J.'s stomach lurched. "What?"

Half doubled over, not looking at him, she said tensely, "I think my water just broke."

Chapter 3

J.J. uttered a string of words he wouldn't use in the presence of a real nun and got another of her fierce black looks in return. This one, though, seemed to hold less anger and more of what he interpreted as mute appeal. *Help me.* Words he was beginning to suspect this particular woman wouldn't find easy to utter out loud under normal circumstances.

He touched on his radio mic. "Katie, I'm gonna need an ambulance out here, ASAP. Uh…scratch that," he said as the woman abruptly sagged against the side of his patrol vehicle and began doing that pant-moan thing again. "Make that a chopper. And give me an ETA."

"I'm on it. Let me get back to you on that ETA…"

The radio went silent. J.J. opened both driver's side doors and waited while Moonshine jumped in ahead of him and clambered across to the passenger seat, then sat in the driver's seat and got the SUV's engine started and the air conditioner going full blast. When he went back to see how his pregnant nun was doing, he found that she'd taken off the head thing— wimple?—and was using one corner of it to mop sweat off of her face and neck. It came as no surprise to him that her hair, which she'd twisted into a knot at the back of her head, was ink-black and also soaking wet.

The radio crackled. "Uh, Sheriff? J.J.?"

"Yeah, go ahead."

"Dispatch wants to know the nature of the emergency. Are we talking MVA trauma or heatstroke?"

"Uh…that's a negative on both. Make that…woman in labor."

"Labor?" Katie's voice rose to a squeak—not very professional of her, in J.J.'s opinion. "Are you telling me this is the *nun?*"

J.J. grunted, being involved at the moment in helping the "nun" in question into the backseat of his patrol vehicle. He watched her sort of crumple onto her side and pull her knees up onto the seat before he closed the door. She was whimpering softly now. There was a knot forming in his belly as he turned his back to her and spoke to his radio mic. "Yeah, well, that seems doubtful. The nun part, not the labor. You got an ETA on that chopper?"

"Uh…that's the problem. Ridgecrest's choppers are out on a multi-vehicle MVA up on 395. No idea how long they'll be."

J.J. looked up at the sun-washed sky and swore. He was pondering his best course of action when his radio crackled to life again.

"I could get you somebody out of Barstow, but it would probably be just as fast if you take her in to Ridgecrest yourself, that would be the closest. How far along is she?" Katie had three kids, which probably made her the closest thing he had to an expert at the moment.

"In months? I'm guessing…nine."

"No, I mean the labor." She didn't say the word *dummy*. J.J. being her boss, but he could hear it in her voice just the same.

"How the hell should I know?" he said. "Her water just broke."

"Yikes," said Katie. "Well, that could mean…just about anything, actually. She could have hours yet. Or minutes."

"Well, don't ask me," J.J. growled. "I'm not a doctor."

"I…am." That came, surprisingly, from the backseat.

He jerked around to look at the woman, who he could see was now half propped up on one elbow. Her exotic eyes seemed huge in her chalk-white face. "You are what? A *doctor?*"

She nodded, then closed her eyes and sank back onto the pillow of her folded arm. "Well…sort of. I never finished my internship. But I know enough—" she broke off for a couple more pants and groans, then finished with clenched teeth "—to know I haven't got hours."

Grimly, J.J. relayed to his mic, "She doesn't think she's got hours."

"How far apart are the contractions?"

"Hell, I don't know. Seems to me they're more or less continuous."

"Oh, Lord," said Katie. "That's not good."

"If you're going to take me to a hospital, you'd better get going," came the faint, gasping voice from the backseat, at the same time Katie's voice on the radio was saying, "Well, you'd better hurry. I'll let Ridgecrest know you're coming."

"Ten-four." He put the SUV in gear and made a U-turn, tires spitting fine gravel.

"Okay, drive safe." The radio went silent.

He didn't turn on his siren, since it would only make the dog miserable, and there weren't any other vehicles in the immediate vicinity anyway. He brought the speed up to what he considered the maximum for safety, then glanced in his rearview mirror.

"How you doin' back there?"

No answer for a moment. Then, "Just lovely, thank you."

He couldn't believe he was even *thinking* of smiling.

As he drove, although his attention was totally focused on the road ahead, part of his mind kept jumping and skittering every which way, so full of the questions he wanted to ask, his head felt like a nest of spooked jackrabbits. For a long time he didn't ask any of the questions because he couldn't decide which one to ask first. Finally, though, when it seemed one kept popping up more often and more insistently than the rest, he looked up to his rearview mirror and said, "Ma'am, if you're not a nun, what's with the habit?"

Her voice sounded tired, out of sorts and groggy. "No… obviously…I'm not a nun. The habit—and the car—belong to a friend of mine. When I drove the car into that ditch… when I knew I was going to have to walk for help, I thought the habit might help protect me from the sun. You know, like the robes Arabs wear."

J.J. nodded. He was thinking, *Okay, she's no dummy.* But he wished he could see her face, because to him the speech sounded a little too long, a little too glib, like something she'd practiced in her mind ahead of time. It sounded plausible, might even be true—as far as it went. But he had a feeling there was more—a good deal more—she wasn't telling him.

And it sure didn't explain those bruises.

He said, "You ready to tell me the truth about how you got those bruises on your face?"

This time the only answer he got was some loud groans and whimpering cries, which he found both alarming and frustrating. Frustrating, because for all he knew she could be faking, or at least exaggerating her situation to evade the question. But if the sounds she was making were for real…

His radio coughed and Katie's voice said, "Okay, J.J.? I've got Ridgecrest on the phone. Just in case."

Just in case. Swell. He didn't like the sound of that. "Copy," he said on a gusty exhalation, but Katie wasn't through.

"Okay, I gave them what you told me, about the water and all, and the contractions. They want to know if she's feeling the urge to push."

J.J. mashed the button to answer, but before he could get a word out, here came one of those gut-wrenching groans.

"Wow," Katie said, "I heard *that*."

Heart pounding, J.J. said, "Ma'am, are you all right?"

What he got for an answer was a sound that raised the hair on the back of his neck—a primal sound somewhere between a growl and a scream. It even got to Moonshine, who whimpered and licked her chops nervously.

"Ridgecrest says don't let her push," Katie's voice crackled from his shoulder.

"Ma'am, you got that?" J.J. was trying hard to keep his voice calm, and on the whole wasn't displeased with the results. So far. "You're not supposed to push. Try not to push, okay?"

"Okay." She said that in a thin, pitiful voice, like a scared child's. And in the next second, sounding like someone trying to bench press a Harley, *"I...can't...stop!"*

"She says she can't stop," J.J. relayed to Katie. And he was shaken enough to add, "What the hell am I supposed to do?"

There was a pause, and then, "Ridgecrest says get her to pant."

"Pant?"

"You know. When she feels the urge to push, tell her to take in a breath and blow it out through her mouth in short puffs."

"Ma'am? You got that?"

"Yeah. Okay…" Now she sounded like a little kid trying to stop crying.

"Oh, and J.J.? Ridgecrest says that won't work indefinitely. It'll only slow things down, and unless you're less than ten or fifteen minutes out, you might want to pull over sometime soon."

J.J. swore, muttering under his breath. The woman in the backseat was silent, for the moment, thank God. And for a moment, hope flared within him. Maybe…just maybe, she was slackening off this pushing business. Maybe things would ease up enough to give him time to get her to the hospital in Ridgecrest. Maybe…

"J.J., you copy?"

The woman in the backseat picked that moment to start with that awful noise again, causing Moonshine to whine and flop down on the seat with her head on her paws. J.J. bet she'd have put her paws over her ears if she could. He wished he could.

"Don't *push!* Take a deep breath and *blow!*" he yelled over his shoulder, then said to his radio, "Yeah, *copy.* Ten-four." Back to the woman again: "Like this—" And he was puffing like a steam engine, all the while craning to see the backseat in his rearview mirror.

"The hell with this," he muttered, and pulled onto the wide dirt shoulder and jerked to a stop in a rising cloud of dust. He left the motor running for the air-conditioning and got out of the vehicle, telling Moonshine to stay put—not that it was necessary; the dog obviously wasn't going anywhere except maybe to hide under the seat.

When he opened the back door, his passenger raised herself on both her elbows and stared at him, and this time her eyes were bottomless wells of fear. That kind of got to him, more so than the fact that she was breathing hard and her face was wet with sweat so that wisps of her black hair clung to her pale cheeks like seaweed on a drowned corpse.

"Why are we stopping?"

He really wished he had a more gentle and nurturing nature, but in his defense, those weren't exactly qualities that made for a good homicide cop—or probably any kind of cop, for that matter. Still, he tried his best to be patient. "Because you're about to have a baby, ma'am, and I can't be much help to you if I'm driving."

It wouldn't have seemed possible for her face to get any whiter or her eyes any blacker, but he could have sworn they did. "No! We have to go to the hospital!" She struggled to sit up, at the same time yelling, fierce and stricken at the same time, her words tumbling from her with gasping breaths. "I can't have my baby here—I can't. I won't push. I promise—just don't let me—Oh…God!" And then she was doubled up, hands gripping her drawn-up knees, face contorted, making that awful sound.

J.J. looked over his shoulder, then up to the sky, as if there might be some form of help coming from either of those quarters. Which there wasn't. Of course there wasn't. It was all up to him. And he'd never felt so helpless in his life.

The contraction seemed to be passing, thank God. The woman was only sobbing now, which at least was something more like what he was used to. In homicide, everybody did a lot of crying—family and friends of the victim, traumatized witnesses, even the perps, when they got caught. This he could handle.

"I'm sorry," she wailed, then hiccupped loudly. "I can't help it. I just…can't keep from p-pushing."

"Well, ma'am," he said, trying a firm and authoritative approach, "since we are going to do this thing, I guess there's no need for you to stop pushing. But I'm going to need you to do some things, okay? I'm gonna need you to help me out here. It's been a long time since they told me how to do this, so I'm pretty rusty. I'm sure you know a lot more than I do. So you need to stay calm, okay?"

"Okay," she whispered, sniffing. She swiped at her wet cheeks with one hand. "What do you want me to do?"

"Well, for starters," J.J. said, giving her a smile he was sure wouldn't fool anybody, "since it looks like I'm about to help your baby into the world, I'd like to be able to call you something besides 'ma'am.' Could you tell me your name?"

She hiccuped again and gave a funny little laugh. "Rachel. It's…Rachel."

Rachel.

The name sounded strange, coming from her own lips, like a word in a foreign language. The person named Rachel seemed to her like someone she might have known a long time ago, or perhaps in another life. Another universe.

The one she occupied now was a strange, dreamlike world where nothing seemed real and time had no meaning. How long had it been since she'd driven Izzy's car into that ravine, since she'd put on Izzy's habit and set out walking across the desert? One moment it seemed like hours—she knew it *must* have been hours—and the next she felt it had could have been only seconds. Right now she felt as if she was still out there plodding along, one foot setting itself down in front of the other in endlessly repeating sequence, sometimes without any direction from her.

I'm so tired. She wanted desperately to stop, to lie down somewhere. But her body kept pushing her on, forcing her on.

"I want to stop," she said. "I have to rest."

She heard a soft deep chuckle, and the face from the Western movie swam into view. "Afraid you can't do that, Rachel, honey. Looks like you're gonna have your baby right here, like it or not."

What? Here? Ridiculous! She shook her head, adamant, furious. "No. I can't. You're taking me to the hospital. *I have to go to the hospital.*"

But then she felt her body being wrenched out of her control again, and now it seemed it was trying its best to turn itself wrong-side-out. Again and again she was caught up by terrible, powerful forces and was utterly helpless to stop what was happening to her. The only thing she could think of to compare it to was once when she and Nicky had been at the beach, swimming, and she'd gotten caught in a huge breaking wave. She'd felt herself being tossed and twisted and dashed down into swirling sand and seawater, arms and legs going every which way like a rag doll in a washing machine, and her mind, disconnected from her body, had thought, *Oh, wow, I'm drowning.* And she'd felt no fear, she remembered, only mild surprise.

Someone—the stranger named Rachel—was screaming. Belly-deep, grinding screams that sounded like something being torn in half. She felt unbearable pressure, pressure she was sure she couldn't stand another second. She heard someone bellow, "I can't…"

"Shh…yes, you can…you're doin' fine, darlin'…just a little bit more…" The voice was deep and growly, like a tiger purring, and seemed to be very close to her ear.

It was *him* again, the man from the Western movie. He even sounded a little like a cowboy, she thought, with that accent. A little bit like John Wayne. For some odd reason she found that reassuring. She realized that he was holding her, and that his arms were very hard and strong and that his shirt front was warm and slightly damp where her forehead pressed against it. She was sorry when he eased her away from him. She opened her eyes and watched his face as he laid her down. She noticed that he wasn't wearing his cowboy hat now. His hair was damp and there was a groove around his head from where it had been. She wondered what had happened to his hat.

She closed her eyes and whimpered, feeling ashamed, "I'm so tired."

"I know…rest a little bit now, okay? Just rest…that's right."

I can't believe this is happening. My baby, Nicky's baby—Carlos Delacorte's grandson—is going to be born in a cop car. Delivered by a cop!

That struck her as terribly funny. She wanted to laugh, but when she started what she thought was a laugh, tears squeezed from her eyes and ran down into her ears.

"Easy, now…you're gonna be okay," the growly voice said. But then another voice—a woman's voice—rode right over it and drowned it out.

"J.J., Ridgecrest wants to know what's happening. Um… like, what can you see?"

See? "Uh…Lord, I don't know…hold on a minute," J.J. said.

This was all happening much too fast for him. He ran a hand over his face while he regarded the woman, who was now lying back on the seat. She appeared to be crying. He could see her face, with tears streaming down the sides and into her already soaking-wet hair. Other than that, she looked to him like a great big mound of clothing. He knew what he was going to have to do next, and the only thing he could think of he'd have dreaded more was breaking the news to somebody that their loved one was dead. That was the worst. But peeling nun's clothes off a woman in labor was right up there close.

"Ma'am—uh, Rachel, I want you to listen to me, okay? I'm gonna need you to take off whatever you've got on under that gown you're wearing. Can you do that?"

He didn't know what he'd expected—protests, maybe, or some shyness? But she didn't bat an eye. Just sniffled and said, "Okay…" But then she only plucked ineffectively at the habit, like she didn't know what to do with it.

He took a deep breath…heaved a silent sigh. "Need some help?"

She nodded and muttered, "I'm all wet."

It struck him then, that this must be something Mother Nature provided, this temporary suspension of modesty that made it possible for a woman to tolerate being intimately exposed to total strangers. Knowing that she truly wouldn't mind made it easier for him, somehow.

It also occurred to him that the habit made a pretty damn good drape.

Still, it wasn't easy, getting her out of her wet clothes. Especially since she wasn't able to be of much help. She kept having contractions that doubled her up and seemed to take her off into a place where she wasn't even aware of him and what he was doing. By the time he had her shoes off—at least they were good quality sensible athletic shoes—and her wet socks, and started tugging on her slacks, he was almost as wet with sweat as she was.

But he got them off, finally, and her underwear, too. And that was when he ran into something unexpected. When he pulled off her underpants, something came with them—an envelope. It was thick and white and addressed by hand, with no stamp or postmark, just some tape around the edges, the kind used to hold bandages in place, the kind that doesn't irritate the skin.

What the hell? His cop radar was pinging again, this time clear off the scale. A pregnant woman wearing a nun's habit—some kind of disguise, he now figured—clearly having suffered a fairly recent beating, found walking alone in the middle of the Mojave Desert—what was she doing with an envelope taped to her stomach?

He'd have given a lot to know what was in that envelope, but right now he had more pressing things on his mind.

"J.J.? Are you there?"

"Copy…"

"Ridgecrest wants to know what's happening, and so do I." Katie's voice came tensely from his shoulder.

"Uh…hold on…" He took mental note of the name on the envelope—Rachel Malone Delacorte—and the address, a very pricey part of Beverly Hills, then laid the envelope on top of the pile of shoes and clothing on the floor where they'd be out of the way. Then, hoping his hands weren't going to shake, he lifted the edge of the habit.

"Uh…okay, looks like the baby's right there."

"Ridgecrest says, can you tell if it's the head."

"Uh…yeah, seems to be."

"Okay, Ridgecrest wants to know, which way is it facing—up or down?"

Jeez. "Too soon to tell," he said tersely. He gulped in air to fight off the beginnings of queasiness and looked over the top of the draped habit. Smiled wretchedly. "Hear that, Rachel? Won't be much longer now…" *Lord, I hope.*

"J.J., Ridgecrest says you better get ready. Have you got anything to catch the baby with."

Catch the baby? Envisioning a giant-sized catcher's mitt, he felt an absurd impulse to laugh.

"And something to tie off the cord."

"Copy." He leaned across the mound of Rachel's draped knees and said, "I'm just gonna go and get—"

Which was as far as he got before a hand clutched at the front of his shirt, a very small hand with a whole lot of strength to it. *"Don't…leave…me."*

He didn't know why he did what he did then—he sure didn't think about it beforehand. He cupped his hand behind her head and kissed her forehead, then pressed his cheek against her wet hair. Under the salty smell of sweat, he caught something sweet and exotic, like tropical flowers.

"I'm not gonna leave you," he said huskily. "We're doin' this together, you and me. I've just got to get some things out of the back of the vehicle to help us. Okay?" He pulled back and waited for her to look at him and nod her comprehension, then he kissed her forehead again. "Be right back...."

For a moment then, he stood upright in the bright sunlight, pulling in big gulps of hot desert air, trying to get his bearings. Then he went around to open up the back of the SUV and took out the first aid kit and a blanket. When he got back to Rachel, she was lying back quietly, evidently resting, so he took a moment to open up the first aid kit and check the contents. Scissors...cotton balls, bandages, disinfectant...all good. Even a bulb-thing for suctioning out airways, which he seemed to recall he'd probably need. It was good to know some of what he'd learned in his training days was coming back to him.

"J.J.?"

"Copy."

"How are you doing?"

The worry in Katie's voice made him respond with more confidence than he was feeling. "Doin' fine. I think we have everything we need."

"Okay, Ridgecrest says you're going to have to help her push."

"Uh-huh." *Lord, how do I do that?*

"They say when the contractions come you should lift her so she sits up, don't let her lie flat. Gravity helps."

"Gotcha."

"And J.J.? They say don't let her push *too* hard. You, um... don't want her to tear."

No, I sure as hell don't want her to do that. He swallowed down another wave of queasiness and muttered, "Ten-four."

And then, although he wasn't exactly a praying man and it
had been a long, long time since his last appearance in Sunday
school, he sent up a little one: *Okay, Lord, I could use a little
help, here!*

"I have to push again."

The sound of her voice startled him, it had been so long
since she'd spoken. And when he looked at her he got a jolt that
startled him even more. He wasn't sure what it was, something
about the determination in her voice, maybe, contradicting the
stark fear in her eyes, but whatever it was, it made something
kick in his chest, and the next thing he knew he had a lump
in his throat and a big ball of fear in his belly. Because that
went against his grain and everything he thought he knew
about himself, his voice grated hard in his ears when he said,
"Okay, let's do this thing."

Those fearful eyes clung to his, and she whispered, "I don't
know if I can."

The truth was, *he* didn't know if she could, either. It seemed
an impossible thing she was trying to do, and it didn't help
to tell himself it had been done billions of times before, even
under worse circumstances than these. Though he didn't like
admitting it, he felt just plain scared, more scared than he'd
ever been in his life. Going into a house where a guy crazy
high on PCP had just hacked up his wife and the family dog
with a machete and was threatening to do the same to his
kids—that had been a piece of cake compared to this. That,
he'd been trained for. Prepared for. He'd felt confident, capable,
sure. Here, he felt lost. Clueless. What if she *couldn't* do it?
There wasn't anybody here who could help her. Just him.

What if I can't?

"That's not like you, Jethro," he muttered to himself, and
imagined he could hear his mother saying the words, the way
she'd said them to him so many times when he was growing up.

"Who's Jethro?" She was gazing at him, looking confused.

And he was saved from having to answer that when all of a sudden her face crumpled up and her eyes filled with tears and she grabbed hold of his shirt as if she was going over a cliff and he was the only thing saving her.

He got his arms around her shoulders and held her up while she made sounds that turned his insides to ice water. He realized his own body had gone rigid and his jaws were clamped tight, as if somehow that was going to help her, and to make himself stop it, he began to talk to her in a voice that sounded like a truckload of rocks.

"You're doin' fine, sweetheart…that's it…just a little bit more…okay, ease up now…that's it…rest a minute…almost there, darlin'…"

And it became a kind of rhythm, almost like a dance they were doing. She'd grab on to him and he'd hold her, and while she strained and hollered he'd talk to her and tell her how strong and brave and beautiful she was, and it never occurred to him he couldn't possibly know whether she was really any of those things because he'd only known her for an hour or so. Just then, it seemed to him he'd always known her, and always would. Right then, it felt like they were the only two people on the face of the earth—the two of them plus the baby she was trying to push into the world. The SUV's air-conditioning did the best it could, but sweat ran into his eyes and stung like fire, and soaked his shirt and every bit of clothing they were wearing between the two of them. Between contractions he gave her sips of water and poured some on the cloth thing she'd been wearing on her head and bathed her face with it. And it occurred to him while he was doing that, that once he looked past the sweat and the bruises, she really *was* beautiful.

Who in the hell would hit a little bitty pregnant woman? Especially one with a face like that?

He vowed if he ever found out who'd done this to her, he'd give the animal a dose of his own medicine.

Yeah, idiot, and it was that kind of impulse that got you banished to this desert Siberia in the first place. Last thing you need is to get emotionally involved again.

Great advice, he told himself, but hard to follow when the woman in his arms was twisting the buttons off his shirt and soaking his collar with her tears and sweat.

"One more," he told her grimly.

She screamed at him in desperate fury, "You said that the last ten times!"

Then, when he thought neither of them had enough left in them for one more time...

"That's it—I see the head! Come on, baby, just a little bit more...keep pushing...almost there..."

"J.J.," Katie's voice squawked from his shoulder, "Ridgecrest wants to know..." And he didn't even hear the rest.

He was yelling, laughing and...who knows what else, but he didn't give a damn who heard him. "How 'bout that, honey, we have a head!"

"A head? Really?" She was laughing and crying, too, weakly, and breathless with relief. "Is it...is he...?"

But J.J. was too busy to answer her, using his hands and whatever else happened to be within reach, wiping off the scrunched-up face, remembering the bulb-thing to clear stuff out of the flattened lump of a nose and the puffy purple mouth. Then she was pushing again, and he gently held the head while first one shoulder appeared...then the other, and suddenly there he was, with his hands full of slippery, squirmy, brand-new living human being.

He couldn't believe it. He'd never felt such exhilaration in his whole life. Or such awe. And when, after a strangled-sounding gurgle, he heard the first mewing cry, such sheer overwhelming relief.

"My baby…" She was struggling to sit up, sobbing, hands frantically reaching.

J.J. shoved all the habit material out of the way and placed the baby right on her stomach. "Well, Rachel," he said gruffly, as he guided her hands to cradle her newborn, "looks like you have a son."

Chapter 4

Time passed in a haze for Rachel. Fearful and trembling, she watched her unlikely Western movie hero tie and cut her baby's umbilical cord, then wrap him in a blanket and place him in her arms. She had a sense that she might be crying; she didn't know why, she wasn't sad, except that maybe there was just too much emotion inside her, too much joy and relief and awe, and it had to find its own way out.

She could hear the woman's voice on the radio giving her hero—J.J., she called him—instructions from the hospital in Ridgecrest, telling him how to help her to get the baby to nurse, which was important because that would help stop the bleeding. And it didn't seem strange to her at all that this big man with whiskers and long hair and a gun on his belt should be touching her in intimate ways; she barely registered the fact that it was the stranger's rough hand on her breast, gently guiding the nipple to her son's seeking mouth…another hand cradling and dwarfing his tiny, still-wet head. All she could see was her baby's face…his beautiful, perfect round little face, with black hair, wavy like Nicky's. And Nicky's eyes, dark slate-gray now, like all newborns' eyes, but wide open and looking straight back at her.

Nicky...you—we—have a son.

She thought of Carlos then, and began to shiver.

"Here." J.J.'s raspy John Wayne voice said, and he unwrapped the blanket he'd wrapped the baby up in and brought it around both of them, so that her baby was nestled against her skin to skin, naked against her nakedness, the two of them cocooned together inside the warmth of the blanket.

And suddenly, for the first time in a very long time, she felt not only free, but *safe*.

There was a lot more that needed to be done before J.J. was ready to transport his "patient" and her newborn son to the hospital in Ridgecrest, but thankfully, enough of the initial euphoria hung around long enough to get him through it. There was a bad moment or two concerning the placenta—he'd forgotten about that little detail—but they'd gotten through that, and then it was just a matter of wrapping her up, keeping both her and her baby warm and getting them to the hospital as quickly as he possibly could.

For him, it was a strange, tense ride. Even Moonshine kept looking at him and whining, as if she knew something about him was a little bit off. The truth was, he didn't feel like himself. He wasn't normally a worrier, but he kept glancing up at his rearview mirror just to make sure Rachel and the baby were okay. They were both sleeping, exhausted after what they'd been through. He could hardly blame them, even though he'd rather have her awake and talking, just to reassure him.

He still couldn't believe it, the thing she'd done, even though he'd seen it with his own eyes.

He couldn't believe what he'd done, either. What if he hadn't found her? It occurred to him that he might even have saved her life, and her baby's life, too. He thought he could be forgiven for feeling a little bit full of himself about that, but the funny thing was, he didn't. What he felt was *humble*. Because he knew that nothing he'd done with his life up to now, and nothing he might hope to do with the rest of it, was ever going to compare with what this little fragile-looking woman had done today.

He felt something else, too, something he couldn't put his finger on, but it was what made him keep looking in that rearview mirror, tense and alert as if lives were on the line.

It wasn't until they were at the hospital, and he was watching Rachel being strapped onto a gurney, that he realized what it was he was feeling. He watched her hold out her arms for her baby, and the EMT give her son to her and then walk along beside the gurney, kind of touching her, for security's sake. And he realized the stab of pain underneath his ribs was something akin to jealousy. Truth was, he didn't like turning her over to someone else's care. *He* wanted to be the one walking alongside her, protecting her. He'd delivered that baby, he'd saved that mother's life, probably. Dammit, they were *his* responsibility.

And there it was. Whether or not he really was, the truth was he *felt* responsible—for both of them, mother and child. He knew himself, and knew he wasn't going to be able to just let them be whisked away into the E.R. and never see them again. The questions he had…those bruises on her face…

He wasn't going to be able to let this go.

He was chewing on all that in his mind when Rachel looked back over her shoulder and saw him standing there. She said something to the EMT walking beside the gurney, and they all stopped there just before the automatic doors while Rachel turned and held out her hand to J.J. He went over to the gurney and took her hand, marveling all over again at how small and fragile it seemed when he knew she was anything but.

She squeezed his hand and said, "Thank you," with a catch in her voice. Then she looked him straight in the eyes and said, "You're Jethro, right?"

"J.J.," he said, wondering how in the hell she knew his given name. He sure couldn't remember telling her. "Just…J.J."

She studied him for a moment, smiling a crooked little bit of a smile. "No…not *just* J.J. It's got to be J.J. *something*."

"Okay, you got me. It's Fox. Deputy Sheriff J. J. Fox—at your service, ma'am." He dipped his head, since he wasn't wearing a hat to tip, and grinned. "Not thinking of naming your baby after me, I hope."

Her smile came and went, and she said softly, seriously, "His name is Sean Nicholas, after his father—and mine."

"Ah. Of course. Good name." But he felt oddly let down—not about the name, but because somehow the fact that the baby had a father had slipped his mind. Well, hell, of course the kid had a father. And presumably she had a husband, somewhere; now that he thought about it, he realized she was wearing a wedding ring. Which maybe should have seemed wrong, to go along with the nun's habit, except…weren't they supposed to be married to Christ or something? Only, of course, she wasn't really a nun, was she? Which left…the husband.

He wondered if the husband was the one who'd put those bruises on her face. Seemed odd, though, that she'd name her son after him, if he was.

Still, women did some unexplainable things, especially when it came to the men they loved.

"They're both dead," Rachel said.

"I'm sorry." But it was an automatic response, and given the way his heart had jumped when he said that, he wondered if he meant it.

There was an awkward pause, and then J.J. said, "Well—"

at the same time she started to say something, so he stopped and said politely, "Go ahead."

"There's no way I'll ever be able to thank you. I can't imagine what—" She looked down at the bundled baby in her arms and kind of shook her head.

"No need to thank me. Just doin' my job," J.J. muttered, again knowing that wasn't the way he felt. What he was really feeling was gruff and uncomfortable and heroic and utterly fraudulent.

He reached out and touched her arm, then the baby bundle. "You just have a good life—keep this little guy safe, okay?" She nodded. He nodded to the EMT, and the gurney started to roll. "You can call me if you need anything, now, you hear?" he heard himself say. She didn't respond; all her attention was focused now on her baby.

Which was as it should be, he thought morosely. He watched as the gurney was wheeled away into the E.R., and the automatic door whisked shut, closing him out.

Yeah, why in the hell would she need you? He gave a snort of self-mockery and went to clean out his patrol vehicle, which he imagined would be getting pretty ripe by now, warming up in the heat of the day.

He got a large-sized evidence bag out of the back of the SUV and started gathering up the clothing and shoes he'd shucked off Rachel and tossed out of the way during the chaos of delivering her baby. And—oops—there was the envelope that had come off with the clothing, the one that had apparently been taped to her stomach. Damned if he hadn't forgotten about it in all the excitement. Now, sitting behind the wheel of his patrol vehicle, he examined the envelope more closely. The name—Rachel Malone Delacorte. *Delacorte.* Why did that name ring a bell? Where had he heard it before?

Holding the envelope and pondering whether or not he

could justify opening it, he thumbed his radio on. "Katie, do you copy?"

"Yeah, J.J." Katie's voice was higher than normal and breathless with poorly suppressed excitement. "How is—"

"Everybody's fine. Including me," he added wryly, and got a chuckle in response. "Mother and son are fine—just dropped 'em off at Ridgecrest E.R. Ah…Katie, I want you to run a name for me. Put a rush on it." He gave her the name. "You copy?"

"Copy that," Katie said. "When you gonna be back in the office?"

"On my way," J.J. drawled.

What he really wanted to do was go find a quiet spot and a nice cold beer and take an hour or two to ponder the events of the morning. After all, wasn't every day he got to rescue a pregnant woman masquerading as a nun out in the middle of the desert and deliver her baby in the backseat of his patrol vehicle. But since his work day was barely half over, he stuffed the envelope—unopened—into the bag containing Rachel's clothes and took everything inside to the E.R. reception desk. Back outside in the midday sun, he called to Moonshine—no dummy, she'd found a shady spot under a parked ambulance— got in his patrol vehicle and, making mental note to look for a car wash on the way, headed back to his own jurisdiction.

Once again, Rachel drifted. Somewhere in the back of her mind she knew there were things she should be thinking about, planning for. But for the moment, she felt no more capable of controlling the course of her life than a leaf caught in a river's current. And for now, that current was benign, a placid and peaceful stretch after what had been a turbulent, hazardous, sometimes terrifying, sometimes exhilarating ride. For the time being, for the first time in more than two years, she was free of the Delacorte family. For the first time in six months, she was free from fear. Tomorrow, she would think about what to do next. For today, she could allow herself to drift.

I'm in a hospital. My baby and I are safe here.

Lying on her side with her cheek propped on one curled fist, she gazed at her newborn son, now sleeping peacefully, swaddled in a soft white blanket with blue and pink stripes around the edges, a blue stocking cap covering his head and most of his freshly washed silky black hair. A fine, strong, healthy boy, the doctor had told her. Seven pounds, five ounces. A beautiful baby boy. Which Rachel didn't need a doctor to tell her; she could see her son was absolutely perfect.

Nicky, you have a son. You always said…

But her mind, drifting, sailed quickly, almost guiltily past images of Nicholas and settled instead, like a leaf caught in a skein of half-submerged grasses, on the fierce and whiskery face of Deputy Sheriff Jethro—J.J.—Fox.

Who could have imagined our baby would be helped into this world by a lawman? A sheriff straight out of the Old West, one who sounds a little like John Wayne?

She laughed without sound, and was disconcerted when the laughter made everything in her middle quiver like unmolded gelatin. She winced and rested her hand on her disappointingly still-swollen belly, trying to remember what the nurse had assured her: Everything would go back to its normal place soon. And nursing, the nurse had told her firmly, would help that happen faster.

With that memory, Rachel's drifting mind bumped gently against another image: Sheriff Jethro Fox's hands, one cradling her baby's head, the other holding her breast, guiding the nipple to an eagerly seeking mouth. The backs of his hands had been tanned, she remembered, the hair on the wrists bleached golden by the sun, the nails clean and clipped short but not manicured, not like Nicky's. Nicky had cared for his hands as meticulously as any woman.

She wondered why it wasn't more unsettling, remembering the way a strange man had touched her breasts. Instead, she found it a comforting image, and it stayed with her until she dozed.

Katie aimed an accusing stare at J.J. across the tops of her glasses when he walked through the door. "What happened, Grizzly? I thought you were going to shave all that stuff off your face."

"Yeah, well, I've been kind of busy." He took off his hat and sailed it across to his own desk.

Katie held the stare for another beat, then broke out in a grin. "Well, congratulations, anyway." She pulled a cigar out of where she'd been hiding it behind her computer screen and lobbed it at him.

He snagged it and grunted his thanks, as Daryl Fisher, another one of his deputies, pushed off from his desk and tipped his chair back.

"First baby, J.J.?"

J.J. snorted. "Yeah, it was. How many have you brought into the world?" Daryl was fresh out of police academy and liked to think he knew everything. And maybe he did—everything that could be learned out of a book, anyway, which in J.J.'s opinion wasn't much.

Daryl made a scoffing noise and went back to his computer.

"He's just jealous," Katie said comfortingly.

"Yeah, right." J.J. was wondering why he felt so damn crabby. Shouldn't a little euphoria be in order? He nodded toward the computer monitor on Katie's desk. "Anything on that name I gave you?"

Katie gave a little gasp. "Oh—my gosh. Sorry—kind of

got caught up in the celebration." She bit her lower lip to hold back what appeared to be sheer glee. "Hold on to that cigar, J.J., because you're not going to believe this. Rachel Malone Delacorte—I'm guessing that's the new mom?"

"That's what I'm guessing."

"Well, if it's the same one, she's married to Nicholas Delacorte—or *was*." She waited a beat, and when J.J. just looked at her, gave an impatient huff. "Only son of Carlos Delacorte? Head of *the* biggest crime family in the entire southwest, if not the country? *Plus* Central America?"

J.J. swore under his breath. No wonder the name had seemed familiar to him.

"The reason I said *was*," Katie went on, still full of herself. "Remember that shootout in the alley behind the Hollywood Bistro last year? The one where those two feds got killed? Well, you might remember, there was another casualty that night—none other than Carlos Delacorte's little boy, Nicky. At the time, it was thought he might have just gotten caught in the crossfire, since no weapons were found on him. Meanwhile, the shooters, whoever they were, got clean away."

"That case is still open," J.J. said, frowning. It was coming back to him, now. "Didn't witnesses say Delacorte was in the Bistro that night, with a woman?"

Katie nodded. "Presumably his wife, Rachel Delacorte. Supposedly she left the Bistro with her husband, but after the shootout she was nowhere to be found." She turned the monitor so J.J. could see the screen. "So…is this her? Is this your new baby-mama?"

J.J. stared at the screen, and felt his vision field shrink and the world fall away. All sound seemed to be muffled, even his own voice. "That's her," he said.

The photo had been taken at some formal event, maybe a charity ball or premier, the couple posed the way celebrities do for the photographers on the red carpet. And they were as beautiful a couple as any J.J. had ever seen on any red carpet, he dashing in his tux, dark hair wavy to his collar and slicked back on the top and sides, she slender and elegant in a gown made of something shimmery that clung to every curve and left her shoulders, the tops of her breasts and most of her back bare. Her head barely topped her husband's shoulder, even with her hair piled high on her head. Jewels—diamonds, most likely real ones—twinkled in the coils of her shiny black hair and at her ears and throat.

A far cry, he thought, from the woman in the borrowed nun's habit, nine months pregnant and her hair wet and stringy with sweat. But there was no mistaking that heart-shaped face. *Those eyes.*

Katie was saying something. With an effort, he pulled his gaze away from the image of the woman on the computer screen and focused on her. "What?"

Her eyes were grave as they met his. "J.J., if that woman is Rachel Delacorte, then that means…"

"I just delivered Carlos Delacorte's grandson." He let his breath out in a gust.

Even before he said the words, their implications had rumbled over him like a landslide. Everything—Rachel, missing from the scene after the shootout that killed her husband, now turning up pregnant, alone in the desert in a borrowed car and nun's habit, her face wearing the evidence of a brutal beating, afraid to trust anyone, even an officer of the law—it all made sense now. It was pretty obvious the woman had been held prisoner—virtual if not actual—by her father-in-law, notorious crime family kingpin, and had just made a desperate attempt to escape.

Why?

The possibilities turned his blood cold. Witnesses at the Bistro the night of the shootout said Nicholas Delacorte had been with a woman. Although witnesses wouldn't confirm it, and no surveillance cameras could prove it, that woman would almost certainly have been his wife, Rachel. J.J. wasn't familiar with the details of the case, but the wife of one of the victims would almost certainly have been questioned, along with everyone in the Delacorte camp, immediately after the shooting. Nothing had ever come of it, apparently, but if Carlos had been keeping his daughter-in-law under wraps, it would almost certainly have been because she knew too much, was possibly even an eyewitness to the shooting of her husband and two federal agents.

Why not just kill her?

Because she was pregnant, carrying Nicholas's child, the only grandchild Carlos Delacorte would ever have.

And once the child was born…what then? The bruises seemed to indicate there was no love lost between Carlos and his son's wife. Once the baby was safely delivered, he'd have no reason to keep a potential eyewitness to the shooting of two federal lawmen alive.

No wonder Rachel had lit out for parts unknown, even nine months pregnant and probably already in early labor. She'd been running for her life.

J.J. swore, blaspheming in a way that would have made his mother weep. Even Katie, who'd probably heard a whole lot worse in her lifetime, was staring at him openmouthed. He didn't stop to apologize.

"Get Ridgecrest Hospital on the phone," he snapped at her, at the same time he was taking his backup piece out of the desk drawer he'd put it in when he'd first arrived at the Lost Mine Sheriff's Station five months ago. He checked it over, then shoved it inside his boot. It was the first time he'd carried it since he'd left Homicide Division. "Tell them to put extra security on Rachel Delacorte and her baby."

His sense of urgency was like an electric current pulsing through his body. He had to figure Delacorte would be desperate to find his daughter-in-law and get his grandchild back. His organization was huge and far-reaching; he probably had people in every city, county, state and federal law enforcement agency in Southern California. They'd be monitoring every radio call, patrolling every possible escape route, land, sea or air. Carlos *could not* afford to let Rachel get away, and he'd move heaven and earth to find her.

And his only grandchild.

How many hours had it been since that call had gone out about a nun wandering in the desert? How long would it take Delacorte to put two and two together and pick up the trail?

J.J. snatched up his hat and jammed it on his head. He tossed the keys to his trailer to Deputy Daryl.

"Take care of my dog," he growled on his way out the door.

Rachel woke from a light sleep, alerted by something she couldn't immediately identify: faint sounds, scuffles, breathing…small things that told her she wasn't alone. She opened her eyes—a fraction of a second before they were covered by something soft and white.

She screamed, but the sound collided with the thick softness that covered her mouth. She tried to suck in air, and sucked in cloth instead. In desperation now, she struck out with both hands, clutching, scratching, clawing viciously at whatever she could reach. The screams she couldn't utter tore at her throat as her body arched and bucked with all the strength she had left.

Not enough.

She heard voices, muffled voices, low, guttural voices. Brutal, strong hands pressed down on her shoulders. In one final desperate burst of strength, she lashed out with both arms and legs, and heard a growl of pain as her nails raked skin, maybe even drew blood. Then…the loud crash of something being overturned, the sharp *thwack* of heavy plastic hitting the vinyl tile floor. It was a sound that sent horror ricocheting through her brain, because she knew exactly what it was: The bassinet and cart her newborn son slept in, close beside her bed.

My baby! Jethro—help!

It was her last thought before the darkness came.

J.J. had never driven so fast in his life. Not so fast as to be out of control, though; after nearly going airborne through a dip, he had to keep reminding himself that he was no good to anybody dead, or spun out and stuck in a sandy gully somewhere. He drove with full lights and siren, heart thumping, eyes glued to the road ahead, hands glued to the wheel, ears tuned in to any reports that came in over his radio. No reports of any disturbances at Ridgecrest Hospital, though. So far, so good. Maybe he'd get there in time.

He had to slow down coming into the town of Ridgecrest, what with traffic and stoplights, and drivers who evidently had no clue they were supposed to pull over to the curb for emergency vehicles with flashing lights and sirens. It was as he was approaching an intersection with the traffic signal against him, slowing to make his way around bewildered drivers who had stopped in the middle of whatever lane they happened to be in, that he saw, coming along the cross street, a whole line of cop cars, both city and county, lights flashing and sirens blaring, slowing now to make the turn. Heading, evidently, in the same direction he was.

His heart rate kicked up several notches. He waited, swearing vehemently and aloud, for the posse to pass, then threaded his own way through the intersection and gunned it, following hot on their trail.

He had a bad feeling about this. A cold sick feeling in the pit of his stomach.

The feeling got a whole lot worse when he turned into the hospital parking lot and nearly collided with a black SUV with tinted windows as it came lurching out of the lot, made the turn with squealing tires and sped away down the street in the direction he'd just come from. Something—call it instinct, call it gut, or maybe just a lot of years chasing down bad guys—zapped through J.J. like a jolt of electricity, and he almost—*almost*—hung a U-turn and went in pursuit of the black SUV. Instead, he drove on in the wake of the other law enforcement vehicles, but with an increasing heaviness around his heart.

Too late, he thought. *Dammit. Too late.*

Chapter 5

Rachel came back to awareness and an overwhelming sense of grief and terror. She tried to cry out, but something cold and hard was covering her face. She clawed at it, and then at the hands that tried to stop her from doing so. She was crying, sobbing uncontrollably. And there were voices, voices saying words that made no sense to her. Soothing words, nevertheless, and the voices, some of them, were women's.

"It's okay…you're safe now…it's just a little oxygen. It'll help you feel better. It's all right…"

But Rachel was inconsolable. "They…took him. They took…"

"No, no, dear—he's fine. Your baby is fine. He's in the nursery. We took him for tests, so you could sleep…"

They were lying, of course. Telling her that just to calm her. She knew, because she had heard them—heard the bassinet fall. It had happened, just as she'd known it would. Carlos had sent his men to kill her, and they had taken away her baby.

The hospital appeared outwardly calm. Sure, there were cop cars drawn up before every entrance, but nobody was shouting, running or shooting at anybody. Nobody was being evacuated, which meant probably nobody was being held hostage. All of which only confirmed J.J.'s suspicion that the perpetrators, whoever they were and whatever they'd been up to, had already fled the scene, most likely in the black SUV he'd nearly collided with on his way in.

I shouldn't have left her, he told himself. *Dammit, should never have left her alone.*

You didn't know who she was at the time, his reasoning self told him. *How could you have known?*

But he had known. He'd known *something* wasn't right. *I should have stayed until I heard from Katie.*

But as he knew all too well, knowing what he should have done—or not done—after it was too late wasn't worth diddly. Now, he was going to have one more life—possibly two—on his conscience.

Along with the God-only-knew how many more that were there already.

He went in through the emergency entrance, figuring the nurse on watchdog duty would probably recognize him from when he'd brought Rachel and her baby in and give him a minimum of grief. She did, and would have waved him right on in, but the two cops guarding the door needed more convincing.

"A little out of your jurisdiction, aren't you, San Bernardino?" one of them said as he studied J.J.'s identification.

"A bit," J.J. said. He was trying to hide his impatience, his urgent need to move on, but the Ridgecrest cops were no dummies.

"Can I ask what you know about what just went down here?" the one with his ID said, glancing up at him while his partner moved in just a bit closer.

J.J. raised his eyebrows and played dumb. "Something happen? When?"

"Few minutes ago someone assaulted one of the patients here." He took a notepad out of his uniform pocket, glanced at it, and put it back. "Name of Rachel Malone. You know anything about that?"

Giving up the act, J.J. ran a hand over his beard and swore under his breath. "She okay?"

"Looks like it," the cop said, giving him a long, close look as he handed back his ID.

"And her baby?"

"Mind telling me what's your interest, San Bernardino? Like I said, you're way out of your jurisdiction." He paused, obviously thinking about it. "You her husband? Different name, but that don't mean much these days."

"Nope, no relation," J.J. said easily. He really didn't want to step on a fellow lawman's toes. If he could help it.

"You the baby's father?"

Why won't they give me a straight answer? Oh, right, he thought, trying to curb his temper, *cops don't answer questions, they just ask them.*

"No," he said through clenched teeth, "just the guy who delivered him. You gonna tell me how he is, or what?"

Her room seemed filled with people. Policemen—except one was a woman—asking questions, taking pictures, writing notes, talking on their radios or cell phones. Nurses talking to each other in low voices; Rachel could hear them talking about her but didn't care. She didn't care about anything, she was sunk so deep in pain and despair. Pain gripped her like a vise, and it was worse than anything she'd ever known, worse than childbirth, worse than the night Nicky died. She could only wrap her arms around herself and curl herself around the pain, too full of pain even for breath. The nurses kept trying to put the oxygen mask over her face, but she didn't want it. She didn't want to breathe, didn't want to live.

My baby's gone…

Murmuring in the hallway…the nurse's voice, speaking plainly, sounding distressed: "We've told her her baby's fine, but she won't believe us."

"Then why don't you just go and get him and let her see for herself?"

That voice…with an accent…sounding a lot like John Wayne.

The nurse again: "We thought…he's still being monitored… so many people…"

"Too many people? So clear 'em out. Come on, guys, that's enough. You can do this later. Can't you see the lady's had about all she can take?"

She lifted her head and gave a hoarse cry, cried out his name. "Jethro?" It was all she could manage; her throat was raw from weeping.

She tore off the oxygen mask, and this time no one stopped her. She watched him come toward her, swimming his way through people, nurses and policemen, all making for the door now, though in no particular hurry. Then he was beside her, and she just naturally lifted her arms to him and he gathered her in, tenderly, as if he understood how wounded she was. As she clung to him, shaking, she felt his hand cradle her head against him, felt his body tense as his head turned, and his voice rumbled next to her ear as he called over his shoulder, "Somebody go get that baby—*now.*"

She heard a nurse say huffily, from somewhere distant, "Well, I'll have to ask the doctor.…"

And John Wayne's voice grating, "You just do that, sweetheart."

Then all was still. She heard only the thumping of a strong heartbeat against her ear, and felt peace settle around her like a soft warm blanket.

J.J. didn't try to utter comforting words or in fact make any sound at all, just settled himself on the bed beside her and held her tightly, and after a few minutes he felt the tremors and tension in her body ease. Her head stirred against his hand, and he moved that hand to her shoulder, giving her the option to pull away from him if she wanted to.

Which she evidently didn't. She nestled her cheek more closely against his chest and tightened her arms around him. She sighed, and after a moment, sniffed loudly, then whispered, "He's really okay? Tell me the truth."

J.J. uttered a garbled sound, cleared his throat and said, "Yeah, he is."

A shudder ran through her. "I heard the bassinet fall. I thought—"

"He wasn't in it. I guess they'd taken him to the NICU for observation, or something. Just to be on the safe side. You know—since he was born in, uh, less than ideal circumstances."

"I was asleep. And then…" Her voice was muffled and liquid, and she turned her face against his shirt as if to shut out terrible images.

"Did you see who it was who attacked you? Was it Carlos's men?"

"Who else would it be?" she said angrily, then made a small sound, a gasp, and jerked away from him, wiping her cheeks with her fingers. Above them, her eyes were huge and frightened as they searched his face. "How did you— How do you know that?"

He was saved from having to answer her by a discreet knock on the door. He called, "Come in," and the door opened.

A nurse entered slowly, smiling, bringing with her a rolling stainless steel cart which carried a clear plastic box. Inside the box, all wrapped up like a miniature mummy with a little blue stocking cap on his head, was the infant he'd last seen naked and sticky and swathed in one of his own emergency blankets. "I brought your baby," she sang softly.

J.J. got out of the way and Rachel scooted back against the pillows and watched with he could only call *hunger* while the nurse wheeled the cart right up next to the bed. She never took her eyes off that baby, not for a second, and watching her, J.J. got an achy feeling in his throat. Surprised the heck out of him, too. But the truth was, he'd never seen anything quite like the look on Rachel's face when the nurse put that baby in her arms. As embarrassing as it was to find himself all choked up over something so sappy, he couldn't tear his eyes away from it. No way around it—it really was beautiful, and come to think of it, right then he thought *she* was probably the most beautiful woman he'd ever seen.

It was while he was standing there watching Rachel Delacorte cuddle and coo over her son, and thinking how beautiful she was, that it hit him.

What he was looking at was nothing less than his own redemption.

It must have been there in the back of his mind all along, he thought, and was maybe the reason he'd raced like a crazy man trying to get to her in time to save her life. What he had here was in all probability an eyewitness to the unsolved murder of two federal agents. If he could get her to tell what she knew…if he could convince her to testify—and keep her alive long enough to testify—he could close this case. And if he could close this case…if he could close one of the biggest open murder cases in the country in years…well, that ought to be enough to get him his old job back, shouldn't it? Yeah… and he could finally get out of this godforsaken hellhole and back to being a homicide detective where he belonged.

But it wasn't the time to start talking to her about testifying in open court against a murdering mobster. First, he was going to have to get her to trust him. Which, he realized, might not be all that easy.

Assured now that her baby was safe and sleeping in her arms, she lifted her eyes once more to him. And it didn't make him happy to see that they were filled with questions, suspicion…fear. He told himself it was no different from what he was used to dealing with, and the only reason he minded was because it meant his job—getting her to roll over on her mobster in-laws—would be that much tougher. He tried to ignore flashbacks to the way she'd been with him a few hours earlier, when he'd held that baby in his own two hands, all squirmy and slippery and *alive,* heard him take that first breath, make that first sound, then placed him on his mother's belly and guided *her* hands to touch him, cradle him. Tried to ignore the regret he felt now, remembering it all. The way she'd trusted him then. Trusted him in a way nobody had ever trusted him before. The truth was, he'd liked the feeling, and losing it—well, he hadn't expected to mind it this much.

"How did you know?" Her voice was low and tense, and her eyes weren't giving him any quarter. "About Carlos. How could you know?"

"I'm a detective—it's what I do," he said dryly, and instantly regretted it. Stonewalling was automatic for him, but she didn't need that; she needed the truth.

He took a step closer and felt worse than he'd thought possible when she shrank back into her pillows, away from him. He stopped and held up his hand. "Look, it's not what you think. I saw the envelope, okay? The one you were hiding under your clothes. When you, uh, when I helped you take off your clothes in the car. Remember?" He hoped reminding her of the fact that he'd helped her might buy him points, ease her mind. But she didn't say anything, just watched him, tense and still, the way he imagined she might keep her eyes on a rattlesnake she'd come upon unexpectedly, coiled up in her path.

He moved another step closer. At least this time she didn't flinch, which he considered progress.

"Anyway, I saw your name on the envelope. After I left you here at the hospital, I had my office run your name." She closed her eyes in what looked like defeat, and he added with a sympathetic smile, "Hey, like I told you, I'm a detective— well, used to be, anyway, and I am still a cop." He paused, then added gently, "It's my job, Rachel. Really. Among other things, I wanted to see if there was anybody we needed to notify."

Her eyes flew open and she gave a sharp gasp. "You didn't—"

"No. No, I didn't. And whatever you might be thinking, I'm not the reason those goons found you. Your father-in-law probably had his people monitoring police band radio all over the Southwest. I imagine they had you made when the first call came in about a nun wandering in the desert. That's not exactly something you hear every day, you know."

She hesitated, then nodded, and he saw a tear slip between her lashes and run down her cheek. "He'd know about the nun's disguise. And Carlos has people everywhere," she whispered hopelessly. "It really wouldn't surprise me if you turned out to be one of them."

"Well, I'm not," J.J. growled. "That I can promise you. Look, think about it. If I'd wanted to harm you and take your baby, I could have left you out there in the desert to die."

She stared at him for a long moment, then shook her head and whispered, "I was so stupid. Stupid to think I could escape from Carlos Delacorte." She brushed at her cheek as she gazed down at the sleeping baby. "No matter where I go, or what I do, he'll find me. I'm never going to be free of him…or safe."

"Now that," said J.J., settling himself on the bed beside her, "is where you're wrong."

Rachel had to catch her breath, then, a tiny hiccup that was half laugh, half sob. All that was missing, she thought, was for him to call her "little lady." Classic Duke Wayne.

"What?" His smile was wry, almost uncertain, and she found that unexpectedly endearing.

"What?" she shot back to him.

"You looked like you were about to smile."

She looked down at her baby, hoping to hide the tears that flooded unexpectedly into her eyes. Hoping to hide the smile that came with them. "You just reminded me of something, that's all," she whispered. "Someone."

"Your husband?" His voice sounded stiff, diffident.

"No," she said, letting the smile come. "John Wayne."

He gave a snort of surprised laughter. "I remind you of *John Wayne?*"

She looked up at him. "Yeah, you do. Not the way you look—more like…the way you talk. Sometimes." And she couldn't stop a little gasp of surprise as his fingers brushed her cheek.

"John Wayne makes you cry?" His voice was gentle now, the way she remembered it had been…before.

She pulled away from his touch, shaking her head, self-conscious, wishing she hadn't mentioned it. "No, it's just… you know, emotions, I guess." She tried to wave it away with a gesture. "Hormones, maybe?"

"Understandable."

He waited, silent and watchful, and after a moment she gave a self-conscious laugh and heard herself say, "When I was a little girl…" She thought, *I can't believe I'm telling him this. Five minutes ago I thought he was one of Carlos's men, come to kill me.* But the words didn't stop.

"I was very young when my grandmother brought me to

this country. It was a huge change, and I didn't even know the language. I was lost and scared. She used to sit with me and hold me and we wouldn't talk, just watch old Western movies together. I think John Wayne was our favorite." She paused, expecting questions, but he only watched her and waited in that intent way he had, and after a moment she went on, but with more confidence now, maybe because he was such a good listener.

"I'm, um…half Vietnamese. My mother left Vietnam with her family after Saigon fell—they were among the 'boat people'—you probably heard of them. They were some of the lucky ones, because a U.S. Navy ship picked them up and took them to the Philippines. That's where my mother met my father. His name was Sean Malone, and he was stationed there. He was in…I guess you call them 'special ops' now, but anyway, he was killed there, somewhere in Southeast Asia—Cambodia, I think—when I was just a baby. Then my mother died when I was about two, and her family didn't want a half-breed child, so they put me in an orphanage. And…that's where I was when my grandmother found me. It took her two years, but she was finally able to bring me to America to live with her. She lived in Hollywood. Her name was Elizabeth." Her throat had closed up, the way it always did when she spoke of her grandmother, even after all this time, and she could only whisper her name.

"Was?" J.J. prompted softly, in a way that made her try to go on.

She kept her eyes fixed on her slumbering baby's face, and drew a steadying breath. "She died three years ago. It was right before I met Nicky. In fact…"

He finished the thought for her. "Maybe you were looking for someone to fill a gap?"

She let another breath go in a soft hiss. "Yes. Maybe. I've wondered…lately. I know I was very angry at the time.

Because it was cancer that killed my grandmother, and maybe I felt medical science had failed her and I didn't want to be a part of it." She looked up at him and said with soft vehemence, "Cancer makes me *angry*. It's just so...*wrong*. You know?"

He nodded, and his smile was both sympathetic and wry. "I know what you mean. But cancer doesn't make me angry. Cancer is what it is, it doesn't make a conscious decision to ruin someone's life." He paused, then added in a hardened voice, "What does it for me is predators."

"Predators?"

"Yeah, the two-legged kind."

"Like..." Like Carlos, she thought. *But not Nicky. At least he wasn't like that.*

"People who prey on the weak and innocent." The glint in his eyes reminded her of The Duke again. It also made a strange shiver run through her body. She wondered if he noticed it, because he immediately lightened his voice and his face softened with a smile. "I mentioned I used to be a homicide detective. Guess that's why."

"Used to be?" she asked with maybe too much eagerness, glad to have the conversation turned away from her own past. "What happened, did you burn out?"

"No—" He stopped, thinking about it, then made a dismissive gesture. "Hell, I don't know, I suppose that could have had something to do with it. Maybe. Anyway, it's too long a story to get into now. Right now, what we need to do is get you to a safe place."

Safe. She felt a lurching sensation in her stomach, and a clammy chill flooded her skin. She'd actually forgotten, for those few moments, talking with Sheriff Jethro Fox who reminded her somehow of John Wayne. Forgotten that Carlos's men had come to kill her, and very nearly succeeded. It came back to her now, that awful sensation of fighting for breath and finding none...of hearing her baby's bassinet crash to the floor…of knowing she was going to die, and there was nothing she could do to save herself, or her son. Horror seized her. She felt as if she was falling, falling, tumbling from a great height.

"Please," she gasped, and felt someone—J.J.—lifting her baby from her arms. She relinquished him—no, thrust him from her—in desperate panic.

Then she was struggling to get out of bed, under a powerful compulsion to *run,* to *flee,* and strong arms were holding her again, holding her tightly while she shivered and shivered. And this time there was such a sense of familiarity about being in that place, in those arms, that she stopped shivering almost immediately. And the thought shown warm in her mind like a welcome-home lamp: *Here I am safe.*

"This is getting to be a habit," J.J. said gruffly to the air above Rachel's head. The odd thing was, he didn't mind, and even felt a sense of regret when she moved away from him, wiping her eyes. He suspected she'd keep moving farther away, the more she healed and got back to her normal self. Which was the way it should be.

"Feel better now?"

She nodded, but couldn't seem to look straight at him. Her eyes darted here and there, like those of a cornered animal. "I'm sorry, I don't know what—it all just sort of hit me again."

"That's pretty normal," he said easily, reassuring her. "Flashbacks. You'll probably get them a few more times. It's a pretty big shock to the system to have somebody try to kill you."

She gave a watery laugh. "I guess you'd know. You must run into this kind of thing a lot in your line of work."

"Not so much, considering most of the victims I run into— sorry, *ran* into—didn't survive to have flashbacks. You'd be one of the lucky ones."

He could see her looking thoughtful. Then she nodded and released breath in a sigh. "You said, 'someplace safe.' I don't even know where that is."

"Do you mind my asking—where were you going when you ran away from Carlos? You must have had some place in mind when you set out across a few hundred miles of California desert."

She gave her head an emphatic shake. "No—I was just running—" she tried to look him in the eye but couldn't hold it more than a second or two "—to get as far away as I could, as fast as I could."

Okay, so she was maybe the world's worst liar. *And still doesn't trust me all the way.*

It wasn't the time to call her on it, so he let it go—for now. "Well," he said, lapsing into the accent of his North Carolina roots, "we'll figure that all out in a bit. Right now, I'm getting you out of this place. You can't stay here, since Carlos knows where you are, and if he wants to kill you bad enough he'll find a way to do it."

"Then where—"

"For now," J.J. drawled, "soon as they'll let me, I'm taking you home. With me."

The next evening, driving through the desert with Rachel asleep in the seat beside him, her baby in the back in the car seat the hospital had made him go and buy before they'd let him take him, he kept running over it in his mind, asking himself if he was really doing the right thing—the best thing. For *her.* For him, sure, no question. But for Rachel and her baby, it wasn't so clear. Was he just being a single-minded, selfish jackass?

Well, probably. But in spite of that he kept coming back to the conclusion that taking Rachel into his protective custody was the only way he could keep her safe. Keep an eye on her. Yeah, his place wasn't much, but the only people on the planet who knew the exact location of his trailer were Katie and Deputy Daryl. Katie, he'd trust with his life. Daryl, though…

Well, hell. He scowled at the ribbon of blacktop stretching ahead of him while he went back and forth about Daryl in his mind, wondering just how far he could really trust his own deputy. Wondering if Rachel's paranoia about her father-in-law's reach into law enforcement might be contagious.

Beside him, Rachel came awake with a guilty start, the way people do when they've fallen asleep in a moving vehicle. She looked over at him, then twisted around to check on her baby before she faced front again, pushing her hair away from her face with both hands. "Is it much farther?"

"A ways," he said, feeling guilty, now. The hospital hadn't been happy about releasing her and her baby so soon, and it was probably only the fact that she'd almost been killed while in their facility that had made them give in to his request. More concern for the hospital's liability than their patient, J.J. thought, but then, he was inclined to be cynical. "Are you—do you need to stop?"

She shook her head and gave him a wry smile. "No—just wondering. A little sore, you know?"

"To be honest, no, I don't know," he said, glancing at her. "So you're gonna have to tell me if you need anything, okay?"

"No kids?"

"Nope."

"Married?"

"Nope."

"Ever been?"

He glanced over at her again. "No, and I should probably warn you, my place isn't much at its best, and when I left yesterday morning to check out a report of a woman—a nun—walking around all by herself in the desert, it was kind of in a hurry. I haven't been home since, so…be prepared, okay?" He glared at the road ahead. "Anyway, it's just temporary, until I figure out what I'm gonna do with you. At least it's safe. Should be, anyway, since only a couple people even know how to find it, and the ones that do I'm pretty sure I can trust."

She nodded but didn't say anything, and after a moment he looked over at her again. "If you don't mind my askin', how'd you get mixed up with the Delacorte family in the first place?"

She shook her head and he wasn't sure she'd answer him. But then she leaned her head back against the seat and said, "It was at college—UCLA." She cleared her throat and her voice grew firmer. "I was finishing medical school—my last term. Nicky was in my psych class."

He made a snorting sound; it seemed an unlikely major for a mobster's son.

She glanced at him, then hitched in a breath and plowed on. "Anyway…by the time I graduated, my grandmother had died and we were, uh, together. I started my internship, but—"

"Did you give up on your medical career because you wanted to, or because *he* wanted you to?"

She was silent for a moment, which he considered an answer, probably the true one no matter what she told him.

He expected her to be defensive, so she surprised him when she drew a breath and said thoughtfully, "I don't know, now. At the time it seemed…I felt like my relationship with Nicky was so consuming, it didn't seem to leave any time or energy for anything else. So, when he suggested—"

"Suggested?"

The breath came out in a gust. "He didn't understand why I felt I needed to work, when he was so…wealthy. And as I said, my grandmother had died and I wasn't even sure I wanted to be a doctor anymore. So, when he brought it up, it seemed like the right thing to do. At the time. So…I dropped out."

Gave in, is what he thought. Caved. Knuckled under. He thought he was beginning to get a pretty clear picture of Spoiled Nicky the Mobster's Son.

"Everything happened so fast. The next thing I knew, I was married, and then I was pregnant…then Nicky got shot." Her voice had thickened, and when J.J. looked over at her, he caught a glimpse of tears glistening on her cheek. "He didn't have anything to do with his father's business. He'd promised me…"

"And you believed him? Nicholas Delacorte was the only son of the head of an organized crime syndicate roughly the size of New Jersey," J.J. said roughly, angry all of a sudden without really knowing why. "You're kidding yourself if you think he somehow managed to keep his hands squeaky clean. Didn't you ever see *The Godfather?* If he wasn't involved yet, trust me, it was only a matter of time."

There was a little silence, and then she opened her eyes and said without looking at him, "Have you ever been in love, Jethro?"

"Many times," he said dryly, and she surprised him with a watery-sounding laugh. Out of the corner of his eye he saw her brush the tears from her cheeks and sit up straighter.

"Doesn't seem like there would be that many opportunities, out here in the desert."

It was his turn to laugh without much humor in it. "No, there aren't. Just another reason why I love it here so much."

He could feel her studying him. After a moment she asked, "If you don't like it, why are you here?"

"Long story."

"Well—" she held up both hands, gesturing at the barren landscape and the road stretching ahead of them as far as they could see "—looks like we've both got time." He could feel her eyes on him again—those exotic, black-almond eyes. "Unless," she added with a hint of a sly smile, "it's something you're terribly ashamed of."

"Oh, yeah," he growled, "it's definitely that."

"I'm sorry," she said quickly, and looked away, as if it embarrassed her to have stumbled upon his closet full of skeletons. Like a curious—or nosy—little girl, belatedly remembering her manners.

What the hell, he thought. He wanted her to trust him, didn't he? Maybe if he came clean with her it might inspire her to do the same.

So he blew out a breath and scrubbed at his beard stubble, and finally said, "I told you how I feel about predators." She nodded. "Okay, well, because of me, there's one out there somewhere who should have been locked up. Put in a cage where he couldn't hurt another innocent child."

Even through the growth of beard she could see the muscles bunch in his jaw, and knew he must be clenching his teeth—hard. After a moment she said in a low voice, "Okay, I don't understand."

"It's not that complicated. The guy was the worst kind of predator, the kind that preys on children—in particular, little girls." His voice was tight…harsh. Rachel could feel her heart tap-tapping in her loose, quivery belly, and pressed her fist against it while she waited for him to go on. "I had him for the kidnapping and murder of a six-year-old girl. Had him in custody. And I let my personal feelings override my professional judgment. As a result—" He let out an explosive breath. "As a result, he was released on a technicality. Promptly lit out for parts unknown. Now he's gone. Vanished. In the wind."

"What did you do?" Her voice was barely audible. "I can't imagine—"

"Oh, I got…physical. Rough with him. You know—slammed

him up against a wall, I think." He glanced at her briefly, but long enough for her to see the anger, guilt and anguish in his eyes. "He taunted me with what he'd done to that little girl— details. And I lost it. But that's no excuse. Maybe the miserable freak was hoping I'd kill him—put him down like a mad dog, you know? But I shouldn't have lost control. No excuses. Because of what I did that animal is out there somewhere, and sooner or later he's going to do what he does, because that's what they always do, and some other little girl is going to suffer and die and her entire family's lives are going to be destroyed. And that's on me. Innocent people will suffer for what I did."

"But," Rachel said softly, "you are suffering, too. Aren't you?"

He gave a huff of painful laughter as he looked at the expanse of darkening desert all around them. "Every day," he growled. "Every day."

"I don't just mean because you're out here in the desert, now, and you hate it—I'm assuming you being here has something to do with what happened?"

"Yeah, something."

"But that's not the worst part, is it?" He didn't look at her, or reply. "I think you must think about it…live with it, every day. And at night you probably—"

"Jeez, what are you now, my shrink?"

"I'm sorry," she said, because she could see by the stiffness in his neck and shoulders that she'd gone too far.

But I know you have nightmares, Jethro Fox. I know, because I have them, too. About Nicky, and what happened that night. I keep playing it over and over in my head, trying to make it come out differently. And I know you do, too.

Chapter 6

"It's not much," J.J. said, "but at least nobody bothers me out here. And like I said, the only ones who know where I live I'd trust with my life. You should be safe here. For tonight, anyway. We'll have to figure out what we're going to do after that, but right now, you can at least get some rest."

She nodded but didn't say anything. He figured she had to be pretty near worn out, given the day she'd had yesterday, and the fact that nobody ever really gets to rest in a hospital. She'd fallen asleep again, once the talking stopped, until they'd had to stop a ways back when the baby woke up and started fussing so she could nurse him. It was an odd experience for J.J.—definitely a first for him—sitting in the darkness with only the sounds of the desert wind and the occasional yip of a coyote outside the car, and inside, the soft, wet sounds a hungry baby made, nursing at his mother's breast.

Now, though, she was sitting up straight and alert, staring ahead at the silhouette of his trailer, lonely against the slate-dark sky. A three-quarter moon hung high and bright, bright enough to cast shadows on the desert landscape.

"Moonshine," she said.

He thought at first she was talking about the moonlight, but then he saw the dog sitting out in the road in front of the trailer, waiting for him. He gave a little laugh and said, "Yeah, and it's actually her you can thank for saving your life." He nodded at the baby, now sleeping again in the carrier in the backseat. "And your son's. I probably wouldn't have found you without her."

She nodded but didn't reply. He pulled up in the bare place in front of the trailer and stopped, but when he started to open the door and get out, she hitched in a breath and said in a nervous, hurried kind of way, "Is she yours? Or, you know…a police dog?"

"Canine Unit, you mean? Nah, she just wandered in here one day and parked herself, didn't look like she was going to leave, so I let her stay. I call her Moonshine because she always looks like she's a little bit drunk, which is pretty normal for a hound dog. Now and then she comes in handy, like she did today. Why?" he added, because there'd been that something in her voice. "You're not afraid of dogs, are you?"

"Not…afraid, just careful." Her voice was without expression. It had a hollow sound in the dark car. He heard her take another breath. "Carlos has dogs. Dobermans. They have the run of the estate at night, and other times—whenever he wants to make sure nobody comes or goes without his knowledge and consent."

"Prison wardens," J.J. said with a snort.

She nodded. "I've never had a dog as a…you know, a pet."

"Not even growing up? What, your grandmother didn't like dogs?"

"My grandmother liked to garden—flowers, not vegetables. Dogs and flower gardens don't exactly mix."

"Ah. Well, Moonshine isn't exactly a pet. She's more like

a roomy, I guess." He shrugged and opened the car door. "Anyway, we seem to get along okay."

He got out, went around and opened Rachel's door. Moonshine came ambling over to give her a good sniff, then sat back and let him help her out of the car. Rachel managed that part okay, but he could see she was having trouble getting her legs under her and working right, and it hit him again, like a slap upside the head, what she'd been through in the last forty-eight hours or so. He didn't even think twice about it, tiny as she was, just scooped her up in his arms.

She gave a little gasp and said faintly, "You don't have to carry me."

"I think maybe I do," he said, and felt her body shake with silent laughter.

"Well, okay then, pardner," she growled in a very bad Duke Wayne impression, which he was pretty certain he did *not* sound like, at least he hoped not.

He made an ambiguous growling sound back to her and carried her up the steps and into his trailer. He put her down on the couch and was heading back out to get the baby when he spotted a sticky note from Katie stuck on the inside of the door saying she'd made up his bed with clean sheets and stocked the fridge with a few groceries. God bless the woman, because those were two things he hadn't even thought about himself.

When he opened the back door of his vehicle to unbuckle the baby carrier seat, Moonshine had to come over and go through the sniff-test thing again. Having evidently given the new arrival her approval, she trotted along at J.J.'s heels right up to the bottom of the steps. There, instead of flopping down in the dust for a snooze as was her usual habit, she parked herself on her haunches on full alert, as if she knew whatever was in that carrier was precious cargo and in need of her protection.

"Good girl," J.J. muttered, and wondered for the hundredth time where the old dog had come from and what kind of stories she could tell if only she could talk.

Back inside the trailer he found Rachel sitting on the couch, hunched up with her arms wrapped around herself, like she was cold. Which reminded him it could definitely get chilly, spring nights in the desert, and she was wearing only a pair of green scrubs the hospital had given her to replace her blood-stained clothes. He set the baby carrier on the floor beside her feet and felt her gaze following him as he turned on the heat, then ducked into his bedroom to find something warm for her to put on.

It felt oddly uncomfortable, having her there, having her watch him. It wasn't as if sharing his quarters with a woman was an uncommon thing, just…not *these* quarters. He hated to admit that he minded that he was living in a dinky, shabby old trailer. Or at least it didn't exactly fit the image he wanted to have of himself, had been accustomed to having of himself.

Not that this woman was somebody whose opinion of him should matter, so why should he care what she thought?

"I'm going to need to buy some clothes," Rachel said when he handed her one of his sweatshirts—he thought an old girlfriend must have given it to him, because he couldn't imagine buying anything that had "Life's a Beach" printed on it. He watched her pull it on over her head and tug the excess down around her hips, and while he waited for her to do it, felt an inexplicable urge to slip his fingers under her hair and pull it free of the neckline of the shirt for her.

"I'll have Katie bring over some stuff tomorrow," he said absently, his eyes following the movements of her hands as she rolled up the sweatshirt's way-too-long sleeves.

She looked up at him, and he felt a weird swimming sensation, looking down into those deep dark eyes. "Katie? That's the one I heard talking to you on the radio…"

"Right. She's my…I guess they don't call them secretaries now. My administrative assistant—that's it. She runs the office, is what she does. Anyway, she's got daughters. Ought to have something you can wear. Meanwhile, you can wear that, or I can find you a T-shirt, if that'd be more comfortable to sleep in. Probably come about to your knees."

"No, no—that's okay. This is fine."

"Well, okay then. Is there anything I can get you? Are you hungry?"

"No, thank you. I'm fine."

"Uh…you can sleep in the bedroom. Katie put clean sheets on the bed, so I know she meant for you to. So…whenever you feel like it, just…you know, make yourself comfortable."

"Thank you."

Her voice sounded breathy and rushed, as if she couldn't wait for him to go away and leave her be. He couldn't blame her for wanting some privacy, after the kind of invasions she'd had to put up with, and since he'd run out of things to say to her, or ask her, he gave her a "good-night" nod, got himself a cold beer out of the fridge and took himself outside. Feeling like an intruder in his own house, he sat in an old aluminum folding chair beside the steps, and Moonshine came and flopped down beside him with a gusty sigh, as if she was more than happy to turn over sentry duty to him.

He put his hand on her head, took a big swallow of beer, gave a sigh of his own and growled, "Yeah, it's been one helluva coupla days, hasn't it, old girl?"

The dog didn't reply, so J.J. leaned his head back and looked up at the sky, which wasn't showing too many stars on such a moon-bright night. He listened for a moment to the sound of the wind shushing through the desert shrubbery, and for some reason felt a little bit lonely.

He thought about Rachel and what he'd seen her do yesterday, and what he was going to try to talk her into doing for him in the near future, and the thoughts made him feel itchy and restless.

Not guilty. No, not that. Why should I feel guilty? She's an eyewitness to the murder of two federal agents. It's her damn duty to tell what she knows.

He muttered under his breath, a couple of phrases his mama wouldn't have approved of, then reached down and unlatched the guitar case that lay on the ground beside the aluminum chair. He took out his guitar, tuned it up and then cradled it against him and began to diddle around. Just chords, at first, and then the chords sort of found their way into a Springsteen song, one from one of his old acoustic albums, kind of mournful, which suited his mood.

He stopped playing when Moonshine suddenly lifted her head up off her paws, and a moment later he heard the door of his trailer creak open. He set the guitar back in its case and watched Rachel come out, silhouetted for a couple of seconds against the light inside before she made her way down the steps, holding on to the wooden railing with both hands. He got up and went to get her, meaning to help her to the chair, but she shook her head and seated herself gingerly on the next-to-bottom step.

"You didn't have to stop playing. I just wanted to give you this." She held it out to him—the envelope he'd last seen when he'd copied her name and address off the front, the one she'd had taped to her belly, that he'd removed from her yesterday morning along with her clothes.

He gave a little snort of surprise as he took it from her. "Where'd you have it stashed this time?"

He could barely make out her hint of a smile. "Not on me—I don't think it would stick. Right now my stomach's pretty much like a big bowl of pudding. I had it under the cushion in the baby carrier."

"Well, it must be pretty important," J.J. drawled. *Con-*

sidering the trouble you've gone through to keep it hidden—and safe.

She nodded, and when she spoke, she sounded tense. "It—that letter—is what made me think I could finally get away from Carlos. That's where I was planning to go."

He held the envelope, weighing it in his hand. "So...why are you giving it to me now? Does this mean you've decided to trust me? A little?"

Again she had her arms wrapped around herself, huddled on that hard wooden step, and her face was turned away and in shadows. Her voice sounded whispery and exhausted. "Please understand...it's been very hard for me to know who to trust. But—" she exhaled audibly "—as you said, I guess if you'd wanted to kill me and take my baby back to Carlos, it would have been very easy for you to do that. Instead, as you pointed out, I have you—and your dog—to thank for saving our lives. So, since I can't do this by myself and am going to have to trust someone, it might as well be you."

"A ringing endorsement if I ever heard one," J.J. said dryly. He opened the envelope and took out several sheets of paper, some of it heavy and obviously expensive. "You gonna tell me what this is, or let me figure it out for myself?"

"It's a letter," she said, in a voice that was suddenly completely devoid of expression. "From my grandfather, Sam Malone."

"Sam Malone?" He glanced up at her and grinned. "Not *the* Sam Malone, I suppose?"

She stared blankly back at him. "I didn't even know there was a *the* Sam Malone."

"Come on. Reclusive multibillionaire, struck it rich out here on the desert somewhere during the Great Depression, made a fortune during World War II, hung out with the rich and the famous before he dropped out of sight sometime in the sixties. Not as notorious—or as crazy—as Howard Hughes, but in the same general category. Don't tell me you never heard of him. My God, I didn't know he was still alive."

She shook her head in a bewildered kind of way and said faintly, "I don't know if he is."

He stood up and clicked on a switch in a cord dangling down alongside the front door, turning on a string of Christmas lights that looped across the front of the trailer. "From what I recall," he said as he sat back down in the folding chair, "the guy was quite a character. Worked as a stuntman in old Hollywood for a while—knew all the big stars. I think he married a starlet, or maybe it was a folksinger…" He lost the train of what he was saying right about then, because he was studying the letter.

The first page was a cover letter from an attorney, and he skimmed it quickly before he set it in his lap and moved on to the next one. This was a handwritten letter, written on lined paper torn from a cheap notebook, the kind J.J. remembered writing school reports on when he was a kid, in the days before his folks had been able to afford a computer. The writing was old-fashioned and hard to read, but underneath that, on more of the lawyer's expensive paper, was what appeared to be a typed version. He pulled that out and began to read.

My name is Sam Malone, though for some reason some have preferred to call me by the nickname, Sierra, and I happen to be your grandfather. I am a very old man now, and I've lived a full and interesting life, during which I managed to amass a considerable fortune and squander the love of three beautiful women. As a result, I was not privileged to know my own children, a fact that I deeply regret. But this is not the time for regrets, and I can't do much to change the past anyhow.

Since I have outlived all of my wives and my children, it is my desire to share my treasure with my grandchildren, any that may chance to survive me, and it is this last wish that has led me to write this letter to you. If you are not too dead-set against me and would care to come to my ranch to collect your inheritance, I do not believe you would be sorry.

I have enclosed a little map, in case you should decide to take me up on my offer. And I'm sure my lawyer will add some instructions as to how to get in touch with my staff, to let them know…

"Wow."

J.J. looked up, hands full of the pages of the letter, and stared at the small form huddled in the pool of light on his front steps. "Good Lord, woman, do you even know what this means? Do you have any idea what kind of resources you have?"

She lifted her head and gazed back at him, her eyes only dark shadows. "You say he was a movie stuntman in old Hollywood…I guess that would explain why my grandmother liked to watch old Western movies, wouldn't it? He was probably in some of them." Her laugh had a liquid sound. "He might even have known him—the Duke. Don't you think?"

J.J. was trying to get his head around the fact that he'd not only delivered the grandson of notorious crime family boss Carlos Delacorte, but also the great-grandson of Sierra Sam Malone, one of the true legends of the twentieth century.

"Wouldn't be a bit surprised," he said.

Rachel gazed out the windows of the anonymous late-model white pickup truck at the desert landscape sweeping by, watching constantly changing vistas—scrubby trees and shrubs she didn't know the names of set on a carpet of golden flowers, juniper and Joshua tree-covered hills, and beyond them mountains layered in shades of purple and blue, canyons with cliffs carved in fantastic shapes and striated in red, orange, pink and cream, plains strewn with black lava rock from eruptions so ancient their sources had long since eroded away. Evidences of human habitation were few and far between, and often in advanced stages of abandonment and decay. Like those long-gone volcanoes, she thought, they'd been unable to stand up to the ravages of heat and sun and the unrelenting wind.

She was sure some people—Sheriff Jethro Fox for one— would find the desert harsh and barren and soulless, but to Rachel the vast emptiness, the endless vistas and boundless sky spoke of *freedom*. She hadn't truly understood until hers was taken from her how precious a thing freedom was. Freedom to come and go, freedom to speak and laugh and visit, and most especially, freedom from *fear*. She wasn't free in that sense, not yet, but the desert, the openness and emptiness, made her heart lift, made her believe such a thing might be possible for her, after all.

She thought then of what it had taken to bring her to this point, where freedom and a future without fear seemed within her grasp. She thought of the unlikely people who had made her escape possible: the mysterious Sam Malone, her grandfather, whom she had resented and despised as long as she could remember for his abandonment of her grandmother, and the letter holding the promise of a means to create a new life for herself, someplace where Carlos couldn't find her.

Then there was…this man. Sheriff J. J. Fox, the lawman who might have stepped right out of one of the old cowboy movies she and Grandmother had loved to watch. The lawman who had not only saved her life and her baby's life, too, but had given her shelter and protection, and now was taking her in his own private pickup truck to find her grandfather's hideaway.

Her stomach clenched when she thought of him, sitting

across the truck's center console from her, not even an arm's length away. It had been a long time since she'd been this close to an attractive man, so close she could almost hear his vital signs humming, smell his aftershave. And she had to smile inwardly at that thought, remembering awakening that morning to the sound of him swearing in the bathroom next to the tiny bedroom in which she'd slept, and then finding him later in the kitchenette, clean-shaven, with his jaws scrubbed rosy and dotted with bits of blood-speckled toilet paper.

Then…she thought of the way she'd trusted him, and fear clenched cold in her belly. *Did* she trust him, really? Was he being a little *too* nice? Sure, he'd said it was his job to rescue and protect her, but hadn't his job ended when he'd delivered her safely to the hospital? Did his job really include taking her and her newborn son into his home, taking her shopping, buying her clothes, personal stuff—a toothbrush?

What does he want?

It swept over her again—the fear and suspicion and uncertainty. It came back to her like a movie scene on replay, recalling Izzy in her habit, telling her not to trust *anyone*.

Then it hit her.

Izzy! Oh, God, I forgot about Izzy. What if Carlos—how could I be so selfish? What have I done?

"Rachel? *Rachel.*"

The sharp edges of J.J.'s voice woke the big old dog sleeping beside the baby carrier in the backseat, and penetrated the fog of fear inside her head. She turned her head away from the window and caught the glance of concern he threw at her, realizing only then that her hands were curled into fists and pressed against her cheeks.

"You were a million miles away," he said, and the side of his mouth she could see was tilted in a John Wayne lopsided smile. He glanced up at his rearview mirror and said, "It's okay, Moon—go back to sleep." Then he looked at her again, and the smile vanished. "What's wrong?"

She opened her mouth, then shook her head and looked out the window again, seeing nothing but a blur this time. *How could I have forgotten Izzy? My dearest friend, and I just left her there. If anything has happened to her...*

"Rachel." His voice was quiet but insistent. "What's wrong? Tell me. If it's something to do with Carlos—"

She shook her head rapidly, as if that would dislodge the awful images that wanted to invade there. Flashes of Carlos's face, suffused with rage, his hand raised, his fist coming at her. Her head exploding with shock and pain. She drew a shuddering breath. "It's…my friend. The one I told you I borrowed the habit from. She insisted I go—I didn't want to leave her there. I didn't. She said Carlos wouldn't harm a nun, but I don't know. I don't think there's anything Carlos wouldn't do. If he's hurt her—"

"Whoa, wait, slow down." The pickup lurched and Moonshine sat up as he pulled off onto the wide sandy shoulder and stopped. He threw the lever, putting the truck in neutral, then turned in his seat and reached for her. She felt his hands on her arms, her shoulders, holding her firmly but not hard. This time, she held herself rigid and didn't give in to the desire to take refuge in the harbor he offered. Because what she really longed to do was lean forward and lay her head against his chest and have his arms come around her, because something beyond all reason was telling her he had the power to make everything right again. She didn't deserve that. She didn't have the right to feel safe, not with Izzy—

"Come on, now, take it easy, okay? Just take a deep breath, calm down and tell me what happened."

She nodded and dropped her eyes, avoiding that steely green gaze and fastening hers instead on a tiny nick on his cheek where he'd cut himself shaving. Staring at that spot, that small vulnerability, she felt a kind of peace come over her, along with a strange urge to touch the cut place. She couldn't recall ever having that kind of impulse with Nicholas. Nicky had guarded his personal privacy religiously. She'd never have dared to invade his personal space unless he invited her to.

She shook off the distraction along with the dangerous impulse to trust this man she barely knew. Allowing herself to become so dependent on a man just because he'd saved her life once and was inexplicably helping her now was just foolhardy. This was real life, not one of her grandmother's old cowboy movies, and you couldn't tell the good guys from the bad guys by the color of their hats. The fact that J. J. Fox reminded her of John Wayne didn't automatically make him a good guy.

On the other hand…the man was a cop, and if Izzy was in trouble, who else could she turn to?

She brushed at her cheeks and straightened up, doing her best to ignore both the dog panting over her shoulder and the pang of regret she felt when J.J. let go of her arms. "My friend, Izzy—Isabelle—we've been best friends since Catholic school. We went to med school together. I quit my internship when I met Nicholas, but she went on, and she's a doctor now. She works in a free clinic in South Los Angeles."

"And, I take it, this friend is also a nun?"

Rachel nodded. "Well, technically, she's a sister, since she's not cloistered. But anyway, she came to visit me, and she was wearing a habit, which she doesn't usually. But…she was wearing it this time because she had a plan—" she pressed her fingers to her lips to cut off a gulp of laughter that was too perilously close to a sob "—to help me escape from Carlos's compound."

"I'm guessing Carlos is the one who gave you those bruises?" His voice was hard and dangerous, and the dog growled low in her throat.

She jerked her glance toward him, saw the same hardness reflected in his eyes. She felt a little chill go through her. "That's not—"

"Look, I'm a cop, okay? I'm a detective, and a damn good one. I've seen bruises like the ones you're wearing, and they don't come from car crashes. I'm guessing you're worried about your friend because somebody hit you, most likely with a fist. If not Carlos, then who?"

She closed her eyes and let go a breath, soft with defeat. "When the letter came—Sam Malone's letter—I read it and signed for it while one of Carlos's guards stood there and watched me. What could he do—short of killing the messenger, I guess. But of course, as soon as the messenger left, he went to tell Carlos. Carlos demanded that I give him the letter, and when I refused, he went ballistic. He, um…" She cleared her throat and swallowed hard.

Watching her struggle with it, J.J. felt a wave of a familiar emotion that was more anger than sympathy. What was it about women who'd been beaten up, that they so often seemed humiliated? As if it was somehow their fault.

After a moment, Rachel pulled herself together and continued matter-of-factly, "I knew he wouldn't kill me or beat me badly enough to risk harming the baby. He *really* wanted the baby. Nicholas's son." She paused, but J.J. just watched her, keeping his face expressionless, his feelings to himself.

She shrugged and went on. "So Izzy came, we switched clothes and I left in Izzy's car. She'd left some money for me in the car—I couldn't take anything with me—no cell phone, no ID, to make it harder for Carlos to find me, you know? The only thing I took with me was the letter." She looked helplessly at J.J and he saw tears flood into her eyes again. She finished in a whisper, "And…I left her there."

She paused then, gazing at him, it seemed to him, as if

awaiting his judgment. He had none to give her, not even absolution, and wasn't sure why.

Taking refuge in action, he spoke to his hands-free car phone, instructing it to connect him with Katie. He turned back to Rachel to ask for her friend's address and cell phone number and the address of the clinic where she worked. She gave him the information, then turned in her seat to gaze at her baby, still sleeping soundly in his carrier in the seat behind hers, while he passed it on and told Katie what to do with it.

And all the while he was doing that, for some reason he was thinking about that morning, when Katie had arrived at his trailer with her arms full of clothes for Rachel and stuff for the baby. There'd been some laughter and hugs and a few tears on the part of both women, and J.J. had watched it all from across a gender divide that at times seemed to him both unfathomable and unbridgeable. And what he felt then, more than anything—besides frustration, maybe—was *envy*. Here were two women, strangers until yesterday, now beginning a friendship, sharing emotions, tears and hugs, and it was all so simple and trusting, truthful and joyous, nothing hidden, nothing held back.

He couldn't even imagine being that way with a woman. Not even with this one. Why was that? he wondered. Okay, so there was the fact that she had trust issues, and he had ulterior motives. So why wasn't there something so simple as the cop-slash-protected-witness relationship between them? Okay, so he'd also delivered her baby and saved her life and maybe she'd formed some kind of dependence on him that she was fighting…

It was making his brain hurt, trying to figure it out. Why, he wondered, did relationships between men and women have to be so damn complicated?

She turned to face him as he broke the phone connection and put the idling pickup truck into drive. He could feel her ink-black eyes on him but given the nature of his thoughts, was trying his best to avoid them. So, without looking at her, he glanced in the rearview mirror and pulled onto the blacktop highway.

"Okay, S.B.C.S.D.—uh...that's San Bernardino County Sheriff's Department—is going to ask L.A.P.D. to check on your friend. They'll let us know as soon as they know anything." He flicked a glance at her as he brought the truck up to speed. "Okay?"

She nodded and murmured, "Thank you."

Her voice sounded remote, a little subdued, and he thought, *Damn. Now I've probably wounded her.*

She probably thought he was making judgments about her and the abuse she'd suffered.

He suddenly wished it was easier to talk to her about things like...well, things he felt deeply about. He wished he could explain to her how he felt about people who preyed on the vulnerable and weak. Bullies. He'd already told her about going off on that child killer, and sure, he'd had an ulterior motive for doing that, hoping to get her to open up to him in return. But maybe someday he would tell her about the time his dad had backhanded him for talking trash to his mother, and how later he'd found his dad weeping out in the front yard. How he'd tried to slink away, but his dad had seen him and beckoned to him, saying "Come on over here, son, I want to tell you something. And I don't want you ever to forget it." And his dad had laid his big, hard hand on his shoulder and said with tears in his eyes, "May the Lord strike me dead if I ever lay a hand on you again, and may He do the same to you if you ever raise your hand to someone who ain't big and strong enough to hit you back. Because He didn't make me a man to bully the weak. It's only animals that do that. You hear me, son? We got to do better than that if we want to call ourselves men."

But he couldn't tell her about that, and the way his dad had grown taller in his eyes that day, because it made him feel exposed and vulnerable to even think about it. He couldn't recall ever telling any woman about that—maybe not anyone, period, not even his mama. Even thinking about it now, at this moment, thinking he might want to tell *this* woman someday was a surprise to him. That he might consider letting this woman see him like that…well, it was a puzzlement.

He cleared his throat and frowned at the empty road in his rearview mirror. "Reason I did it that way is, I don't want anything to lead back to me, maybe give Carlos a clue which way you went. Just in case he's got your friend's communications monitored." He tried a smile that didn't work. "Not being paranoid, just careful."

She gave a soft snort. "You're not being paranoid, just realistic. I'm telling you, Carlos has eyes and ears everywhere."

"You're pretty sure Carlos can't trace you to your grandfather?" At least this felt like a safe subject to him.

"Well, my grandmother didn't have anything to do with my grandfather during *my* lifetime. At least, not that I know about. And when she died I didn't find any contact information among her papers—no addresses or phone numbers, not even old ones. That's why I thought the letter from Sam Malone might be a way out for me, because there's nothing to connect me to him."

Which probably wasn't true, of course, in this information age, but J.J. didn't point that out to her. The connection would be a matter of public record, it just might take a little while for a determined searcher to ferret it out. At the very most, he figured it would give them a little time to prepare. Because from what he knew of the man's reputation, it was only a matter of time before Carlos Delacorte came for his grandson.

Chapter 7

"That must be it, I think—over there," J.J. said, pointing.

Rachel nodded but didn't say anything. He looked over at her, but she just sat gazing past him through the side window of his truck as they paused, idling, on the rutted and rocky dirt road. Across a hillside strewn with rocks and juniper trees, manzanita and sagebrush and pinon and bull pines, they could just make out a bit of red Spanish tile roof showing between guardian spires of tall evergreen and poplar trees.

She hadn't said more than two words since they'd left the desert behind, and he hadn't, either, content to let his navigation system tell him where to turn even though she had the map that had come with Sam Malone's letter spread out across her lap. Except for the couple of times she'd turned around to check on her baby, still sound asleep in his carrier, she'd sat and stared out the windows. It seemed to J.J. there was something suspenseful about the way she gazed upon the passing scene. He could almost hear anticipation coursing through her body like a beating pulse.

Respectful of that tension in her and tied up in his own

thoughts, he'd offered no comment as the road wound up and over a mountain pass, then down into a fertile valley where fat cattle grazed in lush green pastures along the highway. Here and there the pastureland was broken by flat brown fields where sprinklers offered up lacy plumes of spray to the wind, or tractors crawled along through clouds of dust, carving furrows in the silt. Across the fields, following the curves of mountains lumpy with boulders and steep slopes splashed with the vivid orange of poppies, a thick line of trees marked a river's course, the dense thicket of willows and cottonwoods just now showing variegated shades of spring green.

They passed farmhouses in various stages of disrepair and tracts of modest homes shaded by cottonwoods and evergreens. And a church, a simple rectangle of old-fashioned, white-painted clapboard with its spire pointing heavenward, that reminded J.J. of the game he and his sisters had played when they were kids…fingers interlaced, palms together, index fingers forming the steeple. *Here's the church, here's the steeple, open the doors and see all the people….*

Just past the church, the breathy female voice of his navigation system instructed him to turn right, onto a paved road that arrowed across the fields and crossed the river—a mere creek by North Carolina standards, but not bad for Southern California, no doubt well fed by melting snow this time of spring—on a low wooden bridge before beginning the climb up into a canyon tucked away in those forbidding mountains.

Before long they'd left behind all other signs of human habitation and the pavement had petered out entirely, giving way to the track they were now on, which had led them up and over hills and down through boulder-clogged gulleys, negotiating switchbacks that meandered through fields of yet more boulders adrift in seas of wildflowers: lupine and poppy, owl's clover and little yellow daisylike flowers J.J. didn't know the names of.

He thought now—grudgingly—as he gazed across the hillside at the deep dark evergreen trees standing guard over Spanish tile rooftops, that at least old Sam Malone had chosen a pretty nice spot in which to retire from the world. It beat the hell out of a Las Vegas hotel.

"It's beautiful," Rachel said finally, as if she'd come to some sort of decision.

Because he didn't want to admit she'd closely echoed his own thoughts, J.J. said sourly, "Wouldn't want to have to evacuate this place in a hurry for a forest fire."

"Evidently a cup-half-empty person," she remarked without censure.

He shifted the truck into drive. "Just call it the way I see it."

"Maybe you should try looking at things another way."

He glanced over at her and found her looking back at him, and in the mirrors of her dark eyes saw twin images of himself he didn't much care for. The locked gaze lasted longer than it should have, and when he finally broke it he felt edgy and frustrated and was thinking again about complications.

"Maybe," he said, and drove on.

A short distance farther on, the road curved sharply to the left then dipped into a deep gully choked with willows and bumped across a graveled streambed now hubcap-deep in spring snowmelt runoff. It would be dry in another month, he imagined. In a summertime thunderstorm, a flashflood down the channel would be capable of washing a truck like his, or any vehicle unlucky or stupid enough to get caught trying to cross it, clear down to the river.

And that was just fact, he told himself, and had nothing to do with his cup being half-full or half-empty.

Not far beyond the creek, the road ended at a T intersection.

Directly ahead, beyond a whitewashed rail fence, a grassy meadow stretched away to the foot of a mountainside covered with the same granite boulders and mixed vegetation they'd just navigated their way through. More fat black cattle and a few horses grazed in the lush spring grass or dozed in the dappled shade of new-leafed cottonwood trees. To the right, a dirt road followed the fence to the far end of the meadow and a cluster of buildings shaded by more of the huge old cottonwoods. J.J. could make out what appeared to be a farmhouse and an assortment of barns, stables and miscellaneous equipment, typical of a working ranch.

"We go that way," Rachel said, pointing to the left. Her voice sounded as breathy as the navigation system's, only not so much sexy as scared.

Moonshine, up on her haunches now and staring out the windshield, whined softly and licked her chops, as if she understood they were nearing their destination.

J.J. glanced at Rachel, and because what he really wanted to do was reach over and take her hand to let her know she wasn't going to have to face whatever lay ahead of them down that road alone, he muttered instead to the dog, "Almost there, Moon…"

He made the turn onto a somewhat better-maintained road that ran along the edge of the meadow toward the sentinel poplars and evergreens they'd seen from a distance on their way up the canyon. The house with the Spanish tile roof was plainly visible now, a sprawling white hacienda built on a little knoll overlooking the valley below. Even to J.J. it looked pretty impressive.

Hearing a hitch in Rachel's breathing, he slowed, stopped and looked over at her. "You okay?" He said it without much sympathy, afraid he might show too much.

She nodded, then said faintly, "It's not…what I expected."

"What *were* you expecting—a log cabin? The man's a billionaire."

What had she expected? Rachel wondered. None of this seemed real—no more real than the old movies she and Grandmother had watched together—and so different from the life she'd been living for the past two years.

It seems impossible…everything has happened so fast.

She now realized that from the moment the letter arrived, from a grandfather she'd never known, she must have been in a state of some sort of shock. Then Izzy had come, bringing with her a real hope of escape, and after that events had unfolded so quickly, recalling them now was like trying to take in a montage played at too fast a speed: The desert, the baby and J.J. The hospital, Carlos's thugs, nearly being killed, thinking her baby had been taken…and J.J. again. Now…this.

"I'm having a hard time getting my mind around it." She paused to listen to a replay of the massive understatement, then looked over at him as she amended it. "The fact that I have family, I mean."

"Family? I thought you were assuming your grandfather is dead."

"Don't you think so? Why else would his heirs be called to claim their 'inheritance'?"

"Ah—yes. The letter did say 'heirs,' plural."

Rachel nodded. "Grand*children*. Which means, I might have cousins. Do you know what that means to an only child?"

"I know what it means to the one responsible for keeping you safe," J.J. said darkly. "It's just that many more people to worry about."

As if on cue, from the backseat came an infant's snuffly getting-ready-to fuss noises. Instantly, Rachel turned toward the sound, and at the same time felt a strange tingling sensation in her breasts. She gave a little gasp of surprise and glanced at

J.J., her cheeks warming with embarrassment as if he could somehow *see*.

"What?" he said.

She shook her head and muttered, "Nothing."

But she was thinking that trying to get her head around the idea of having a family, maybe some cousins, was nothing compared to getting it around the reality of having a child.

A baby. I'm a mother. When will it start to feel real?

She wondered if it was because she'd spent most of the pregnancy a virtual prisoner in Carlos Delacorte's house instead of going to visit the obstetrician, watching her baby via the ultrasound monitor, watching him grow from a bean-sized lump with a heartbeat to a recognizable human, looking at pictures of the stages of pregnancy in posters on the doctor's wall. Maybe because for the past few months she'd been grieving for Nicholas instead of visiting with girlfriends who'd already been through it all, shopping with her baby's father for a crib and all the cute baby things, having her friends "surprise" her with a baby shower.

Intellectually, of course, because of her medical training she'd been able to mark the mileposts of pregnancy and monitor her own health and that of her growing baby, doing the best she could in her situation. And as her date of delivery had come closer she'd become more and more frightened and her instincts had focused mainly on finding a way to survive, for both herself and her baby. But emotionally…

She lifted her eyes to J.J.'s and said it again. "It just doesn't seem real."

"Sounds real enough to me," he said dryly, as the unhappy sounds from the backseat grew more earnest, and Moonshine whined nervously. He slapped at the gearshift and the truck started to move again, winding its way between towering evergreens and newly leafed poplars, and well-kept beds filled with rosebushes already pruned and ruddy with fragile new growth. "Let's hope they're ready for us."

From a window high in the bell tower above the hacienda's tiny chapel, keen blue eyes followed the white pickup truck's progress as it slipped in and out of view behind copses of trees and sunny beds of roses. Avidly, they watched as the truck drew to a stop next to the curving flagstone steps. The door on the driver's side opened and a tall man got out, crossed to the passenger side and opened the door.

The watcher's head dipped in approval.

He leaned forward, gripping the window ledge with both hands as the woman emerged, stepping carefully, gingerly, the man helping her. While the man turned to open the back door, the woman stood looking around her, then lifted her eyes to the bell tower. For a moment it seemed as if she was looking directly into the watcher's eyes, but he didn't draw back; he knew the tower's thick adobe walls and the angle of the sun would make him invisible to her. He gave a cackle of laughter.

"Well, Elizabeth, should a' known your granddaughter would be the first. Have to say, though—she sure don't look like her daddy, does she? Our Sean…" He gave a sigh. "I know…I know, I got no right to call him mine, after I gave him up—and you, too. But…we both know what a damn fool I was, and that's water under the bridge."

Turning his attention once again to the tableau far below, he watched avidly as the man lifted the carrier holding his first great-grandchild from the pickup truck's backseat. The kid was sure kicking up a rumpus—he could hear it all the way up here. He had to smile at that—fine strong set of lungs, it sounded like.

Then he grew still, and his old heart sped up a notch or two as he watched the girl bend over the carrier, then straighten up with the baby in her arms. He felt a softness in his chest that hadn't been there for a long, long time.

"There's something about her, Elizabeth. Something that reminds me of you." *The way she moves...I remember the way you used to look, holding our baby boy in your arms.*

A whisper stirred through the quiet, so soft it might have been the breeze blowing in the open window.

Are you goin' out to greet them? She's your granddaughter, after all.

Sam Malone shifted his shoulders impatiently. "In good time...in my own good time."

He heard a familiar cackle of laughter. *You always were a coward, Sam Malone. At least when it comes to emotions.*

Mildly stung, he turned to reply, and was surprised to find the room behind him empty.

But not too surprised—it wasn't the first time.

J.J. kept his hand on the small of Rachel's back as they walked together up the wide curving flagstone pathway to a heavy arched wooden door with black iron hinges. He didn't stop to think why; it just felt right to him.

He could feel her body vibrating—*trembling,* he supposed, was the word he ought to use, but somehow it didn't fit with the strength he knew she had. Didn't matter. Whether she was scared, or just wired up with suspense about this unknown she was facing, he felt a powerful need to be there right beside her, to give her support. Protect her, if she needed it.

"Stay, Moonshine," he said, and the dog lowered her haunches to the ground beside the truck but kept her eyes glued to Rachel and the baby. As if she didn't trust the situation any more than he did.

The front door opened, and a woman stood there, smiling a welcome. At the same time, from down the long drive they'd just traveled a man came walking, with a black-and-white border collie ambling at his heels.

Moonshine got up and shambled out to meet them, on alert, but not as if there was any real danger there. And although J.J.'s cop-senses were on full alert, he didn't get any real sense of danger from the man or his dog, either. Like the dog's, the man's pace was unhurried, and although he didn't appear to be smiling, his face and body seemed relaxed.

Meanwhile, the border collie had trotted out to meet Moonshine, and the two of them were sniffing up one another the way dogs do when they're meeting for the first time and are probably going to decide to be friends. Which meant the other dog was probably a male, J.J. thought, since Moon tended to be a little bit territorial around other females.

Satisfied the newcomers posed no threat, to Rachel and the baby *or* the old hound dog, he turned his attention back to the woman in the doorway. She was holding out her arms to Rachel in an open, generous way, and her smile was warm and wide.

"Welcome, Rachel, welcome," she said, and lifted her eyes to include J.J. in the smile. She offered him her hand. "We've been expecting you. I'm Josie."

Her voice was musical and pleasant. She had a smooth, round face with the broad cheekbones and olive skin tones that strongly suggested Native American ancestry. She appeared to be in her mid-sixties, although it was hard to tell since she had so few wrinkles, and her straight salt-and-pepper hair was cut in a style that was both up-to-date and becoming to her face. She wore slacks and a rose-pink blouse with a collar, and what he was almost certain was a hand-beaded Native American-style necklace. Although she was short, she still had an inch or two on Rachel, and her figure was what he thought of as solid…comfortably mature—not slim, but definitely not fat, either.

She nodded and smiled briefly at J.J. as he shook her hand, before turning her attention back to Rachel and the baby. She reminded J.J. then of the hens his mother used to raise, the way she sort of gathered them in under her wings, clucking to them in a welcoming, mothering way.

"Come in, come in, dear…oh, what a sweet baby…a *hungry* baby, too. Come, I have a nice quiet place where you can nurse him. And *you* need something to drink, too, I'm sure. Do you like milk? It's fresh—we have our own cows—or would you rather have some tea?"

Rachel threw him a look over her shoulder, a look not of pleading or of panic, but of such intensity he knew it would stay in his mind for a long time while he tried to figure out what it meant. Then the door closed, leaving him to deal as he would with the man and the dog.

The border collie was now cavorting in happy circles around Moonshine, who sat placidly, evidently considering herself above such unseemly behavior. The man came on alone up the flagstone steps, holding out his hand.

"Hello," he said, "I'm Sage."

J.J. took the proffered hand and shook it. "J.J."

"You'd be the sheriff."

"That I would," J.J. drawled. He and the other man locked eyes, sizing each other up. Like their respective dogs, he thought, figuring out whether or not to be friends.

J.J. couldn't speak for the other guy, but as far as he was concerned, the jury was still out on that one.

The man who called himself "Sage" looked respectable enough, being clean-shaven and neatly dressed in jeans and a western-style long-sleeved blue shirt. J.J. wasn't sure how he felt about the black hair worn in a braid thick as his wrist that hung down past the man's hand-tooled leather belt. But he had to admit it suited him, somehow.

Sage also had a direct and steady gaze and a firm handshake, but since J.J. had known both con men and murderers with those qualities, that didn't mean much to him. Still…the guy did have a definite—and indefinable—*presence*, the kind of pride and self-confidence that didn't need proving to anybody. And there seemed to be both humor and intelligence in those jet-black eyes.

"Alex told us you'd be coming."

"Alex—that would be…"

"Alex Branson—Mr. Malone's attorney."

"Ah," said J.J.

Sage nodded toward the closed door. "You met Josie— Josephine—she's my mom. She…uh, she runs the house."

"Uh-huh," J.J. said, and waited. It had been his experience that if he left the silences for the other person to fill, most of his questions got answered without his having to ask them.

This time was no exception. "I run the ranch," Sage said, and J.J. saw a flash of humor in the other man's eyes that suggested he probably knew exactly what J.J. was up to and didn't particularly mind. "I have a place down at the other end of the meadow. If you'd hung a right at the T instead of a left, it would've taken you to the original old June Canyon Ranch adobe. That's where I live."

"Anybody else live there? Employees? Hired hands?"

"Not at the moment. Later on we'll have a crew to help take the cattle up to the high meadows. Right now there's still too much snow, so it's just me." The tone of Sage's voice hadn't changed, but the sharp black eyes narrowed slightly. "You got a particular reason for asking?"

"Just curious," J.J. said, then found himself on the receiving end of a waiting silence. *Score one for you,* he thought as he let out a capitulating breath. "Look, I'm sure the lawyer explained about me—"

Sage nodded, his gaze keen and unwavering. "He did. What he didn't tell us is why Mr. Malone's granddaughter is in need of a police bodyguard."

"He's a beautiful baby."

Rachel gave a small laugh that was both agreement and frustration; she was still trying to master the art of putting a disposable diaper on a squirming, kicking, unhappy infant. She shook her head and said, "I just can't believe he's really mine." She glanced up at Josie. "You know? Like…oh, my gosh, I have a *baby*."

Josie laughed, a musical ripple that made Rachel think of mountain streams. "Oh, I do know. I remember how it was when Sage was first born."

"Sage is your son?" She hadn't gotten more than a glimpse of the man as he'd come up the drive, but Josie had seemed too young to have a grown son.

The other woman nodded serenely. Then for a few moments they were both silent as Rachel struggled to get the diaper fastened and the blanket snugly wrapped. When the job was done—more or less, Josie looked at Rachel with raised eyebrows and said, "May I?"

"Oh," Rachel said. "Sure." She stood aside and hovered self-consciously as the other woman carefully, tenderly picked up the tidy package she'd made of her baby son. They both laughed as he instantly turned his face toward Josie, mouth open, like a hungry baby bird.

"Oh, my, I think he needs his mama," Josie said, laughing as she handed back the squirming bundle, and Rachel felt a kind of tremulous relief as she took that tender weight in her arms once more.

How terrifying this is, she thought, *to have this bond, now, that I can't bear to have broken, even for a moment.*

"Would you like to come out and sit on the veranda to nurse him? It's nice there this time of day. There's a comfortable chair—a rocker—I like to sit there sometimes."

Realizing suddenly how unsteady she was and grateful for the chance to sit down, Rachel murmured her thanks and followed her hostess through wide, double French doors. She caught an involuntary breath.

"Oh—it's beautiful."

The house had been built Spanish-style around a central courtyard. In the center of the courtyard a three-tiered fountain flowed with happy music into a pool covered with tile artistically done in a colorful mosaic of flowers and birds. Wide pathways paved with flagstone curved from each wing of the house to the central fountain, and between the pathways, small patches of lush green lawn separated flower beds filled with newly leafed shrubs and spring-flowering bulbs—hyacinths and daffodils and freesias, and tulips of every shade. Peeking out between the nodding heads of flowers Rachel could see the spikes and leaves of perennials that would come later—daisies and iris and cannas and peonies. Adjacent to the covered veranda that ran around all four sides of the courtyard, flowerbeds held climbing roses that clung thickly to the supporting pillars and arched over the tiled veranda roof, tangled with honeysuckle and trumpet vines. Here and there among the foliage Rachel caught glimpses of garden art: an old wagon wheel, a ceramic tiled birdbath, a terra-cotta statue of Saint Francis of Assisi, another of a child, a little boy, fishing. Birdhouses, hummingbird feeders and wind chimes hung at intervals from the eves of the veranda, the latter tinkling softly now in the breeze.

Josie glanced at her, a pink blush of pleasure showing in her smooth cheeks. "Thank you. This is…oh, I guess it's my special place. I love flowers. Here in the courtyard, the dogs aren't allowed and the deer and rabbits can't reach, so I can have all the flowers I want. Maybe I overdo, a little."

"Oh, no—it's beautiful. My grandmother loved flowers, too. She would have loved this…" She had to stop, suddenly awash in emotions she thought she'd gotten past. Hormones, she supposed.

Josie nodded, her eyes kind. "Your grandmother—she was Elizabeth. Sam's first wife."

"Yes," Rachel said, and turned away, looking for the promised rocking chair, thankful for the distraction of her squirming son, whose snuffling, fussing noises were becoming increasingly insistent. She had no wish to talk about her grandmother. And especially not her grandfather—not yet. Soon, she would have to. But not now.

"Oh—here," Josie said, and guided her to the glider-type patio rocking chair, holding her arm to help support the baby as Rachel sank gingerly into the thick cushions. "There— you just go ahead and nurse your little one while I get you something to drink. You need to drink lots of fluids, you know, to make milk."

She bustled off, stepping back through the open French doors, and Rachel was left alone with the wind chimes and the chuckling fountain and the scent of hyacinths steeped in sunshine.

How strange…how unreal it all is.

And yet, she realized, that wasn't quite true. What was maybe the strangest thing was how *normal* it seemed. Because it was happening to her, and that made it somehow normal. Or something. She wasn't able to explain it very well, even to herself, but she knew it to be true. Like Dorothy in *The Wizard of Oz,* she thought. Watching that movie as a child with her grandmother, she'd never understood how Dorothy could accept so easily meeting witches and munchkins and talking lions and characters made out of tin and straw. Now she knew that the unreal, once you are in it, becomes *your* reality.

Which makes all this just one more way station on my yellow brick road. And I'm off to see the wizard, the one who is supposed to solve all my problems....

And the wizard is...my grandfather?

She shook off the notion and the irony of it with a small, sobbing laugh.

She was getting better at this nursing business, she thought as she lifted her shirt and unhooked the special bra, one of several Katie had bought for her. She was able to get her swollen nipple into the baby's frantically searching mouth on only the second or third try. As the baby began to nurse hungrily, she closed her eyes and eased herself back into the cushions. Tears stung the backs of her eyelids and breath hissed between her lips as showers of tingles spread from her breasts through her whole body.

It's almost like sex, she thought, then wondered where the thought had come from. It had been a long time since she'd had any thoughts about sex whatsoever. She thought she'd forgotten what it felt like....

She heard rustlings and quiet footsteps, and opened her eyes to see Josie placing a small tray on the table beside her chair.

"Sorry," Josie whispered, "I didn't want to disturb you."

"You didn't," Rachel said, and reinforced it with a smile.

"I brought you both milk and tea—decaf. And I didn't know if you take sweetener, so I brought both sugar and low-cal stuff—the yellow ones. Hope that's okay."

"That's fine," Rachel murmured, filled now with a sweet sense of contentment, listening to her son make satisfied, squeaky sounds as he nursed. "Thank you."

Josie hesitated, seeming uncertain whether she should stay or leave her alone. She gestured toward the doors she'd just come through. "Is this room okay? It's closest to the main wing—to the kitchen, you know—so I thought—"

"It's lovely—thank you."

"Your friend, the sheriff—J.J.—can have the room right next door. Unless you'd like to have him—" She broke off, clearly embarrassed, and gestured again toward the door to Rachel's room.

Rachel just gazed at her for a moment, comprehension coming slowly to her in her mellow mood. Then her heart gave a funny kick and she half straightened. "Oh—no, no. No." Laughing, she made erasing gestures with her hand. "We're not—no. He's just my—I guess he's sort of my—"

"I know you are under his protection," Josie said, coming finally to settle onto the edge of another chair half facing her. She shrugged. "I just thought, maybe there was…you know—something more."

Now it was Rachel's stomach that did an odd little flip. "Why would you think that? I mean—I just met him two days ago. He delivered my baby—saved both our lives, probably. But…no, there's nothing…"

"I'm sorry," Josie said, that pink blush coming again to her smooth round cheeks. "I just thought…you know, the way he is with you. The way he looks at you. Maybe he feels…I don't know…responsible for you?"

"That's probably it." But Rachel's heart was beating faster. *The way he is with me?*

It came back to her then, the way J.J. had put his hand on her back when they were walking. Was that what Josie meant?

Then she was trying to remember if Nicky had ever done that. She thought of all the times they'd gone places together, appeared at benefits and nightclubs and balls and posh parties where celebrities gathered to play. Nicky had loved to be out among the rich and famous, and he'd loved having her on his arm. But no, she couldn't recall that he'd ever put his hand on her back in that certain protective way. Rather, it was almost as if he'd *worn* her, she thought, like an expensive accessory.

Chapter 8

Josie had fallen silent, evidently embarrassed by her gaff. Awkwardly, searching for a new conversational opening, Rachel tore her gaze from her son's face and said, "So...Sage is your son. Does your husband work and live here, too?"

To her dismay, Josie's cheeks got even pinker. "Oh—no, no, I'm not married."

Now it was Rachel's turn to feel her foot in her mouth. She stammered an apology, but Josie smiled.

"I *was* married. My husband, he beat me." She paused and her eyes shifted slightly, and Rachel knew she was looking at the bruises still visible on her own face. Josie didn't mention them, but caught a little breath, dropped her gaze and went on in a softer voice, "Sam Malone found me walking down the road. I had my little girl—Sage's sister, Cheyenne—she was three, then—by the hand, my purse and a diaper bag with her clothes over my shoulder, and the clothes on my back, nothing else. Sam took us in." She paused again. "He's a good man, and I—" She broke off, and when she continued, Rachel had the feeling it wasn't what she'd started to say. "I owe him everything."

Rachel didn't care to hear about her grandfather's "virtues," but something the other woman had said suddenly struck her. "You said, 'is'? Do you mean, he's still alive? Then where is he? Why isn't he here? Why am I here?"

Josie slapped her hands on her knees and rose abruptly. She sidled away, avoiding Rachel's eyes. "Everything will be explained. Soon. When the others arrive, then—"

"The others? Then it's true—there are other grandchildren? Children?" *I have cousins? Aunts, uncles…*

Josie hesitated, then turned. "Children, no—they all died before Sam—Mister Malone. But grandchildren…oh, yes."

"Oh, please." Rachel shifted her now-sleeping baby to her shoulder and tugged her shirt down over her breast, then began to rock and pat his back in a way that already seemed as natural as breathing. "I'm an only child. To think of having cousins—family—is…well, it's just so exciting. Please—tell me about them."

Still Josie hesitated. Then she smiled apologetically as she gave in to the invitation to gossip. "I don't know very much about them, to be honest. We—Mr. Malone—has never met any of his grandchildren."

"That's…sad," Rachel said, but her voice was hard, a reflection of the anger that was never very far from the surface where her grandfather was concerned.

"Yes, it is." Josie sighed. "He was married three times, you know. And each of his wives gave him a child. The first, of course, was Elizabeth—your grandmother. Their son, Sean—"

"My father."

"Yes. He died in southeast Asia—but of course you know about that. And you probably also know that Sam and Elizabeth were divorced long before."

"I know he left her," Rachel said flatly. "For another woman. An actress."

Josie nodded, and gave another of those little shrugs of apology—although for the life of her Rachel didn't see why she should hold herself responsible for her employer's behavior.

"Well, she was…very beautiful. Her name was Barbara." Josie sighed softly. "Anyway… They weren't married very long, but they had a daughter. They named her Savannah, and judging from her pictures, she was as beautiful as her mother. And very talented. She was a singer—folk music, mostly. But…I don't know, maybe growing up without a father, in that Hollywood scene…anyway, she got mixed up with the fast crowd—in those days they all hung out in Laurel Canyon, those music people. She got into drugs and—" Josie lifted her shoulders "—she died. Of an overdose—suicide, maybe, or an accident. Who knows?"

"That's terrible," Rachel said, her voice hoarse and cracking. "But—you said she had a child?"

"Yes. A little girl." Josie gave another sigh and hitched her shoulders. "We don't know very much about her, except that her name is Sunny, and she lives in New York City. We haven't heard from her yet, but we're hoping."

Rachel rocked in silence for a moment. She was surprised at the emotions this news of relatives she'd never met had stirred in her: sadness at lives cut short; fresh anger at the man who had fostered so much unhappiness. She took a deep breath and prompted, "So…wife number three?"

"Yes—Katherine." A smile flickered briefly. "From what I understand, Kate was…well, she was very different from Sam's other wives. Different from him, too. The odd thing is, he was married to her longer than anyone, and yet it was a marriage of convenience—for both of them."

"How so?"

"Kate was from back east—a very old family, politically connected. Like…they were close friends with the Kennedys, that kind of connected. But their family had fallen on hard times, and I guess she needed money to keep up the home and business her grandfather had founded. At that time, Sam—Mr. Malone—he wanted the social acceptance—and political influence—she and her family could give him, so they got married. And, as I said, I think they were happy for quite a long time. But then, when tragedy came—" Josie lifted her shoulders "—I guess they just didn't have the kind of love you need to weather that kind of storm."

"Tragedy?"

"Yes. You see, like her close friends, the Kennedys, Kate wanted their son, John Michael, to go into public service. And, like so many of the Kennedy family, he died too early because of it. He and his wife, Rebecca, died in a plane crash while they were on some sort of mercy mission in Pakistan. Thank God the twins were too young to go with their parents."

"Twins?"

"Miranda and Yancey. They would be the youngest of Sam—Mr. Malone's granddaughters." Josie smiled. "We're expecting them, too. Soon."

"So," J.J. said, "let me get this straight. Sam Malone has just four heirs—the twins, Miranda and Yancey, and Sunny and Rachel. That's it?"

"Four *granddaughters*," Sage corrected.

"Ah—sure," J.J. said, nodding. "I get it. Long-time, loyal employees—I guess you and your mom would stand to come in for a share of the old man's money, too, right?"

Sage smiled in a way that was hard for J.J. to read. "I can tell you're a cop. You think like one—cynical."

J.J. shrugged. "Tell me I'm wrong."

The other man straightened up and pushed away from the

fender of J.J.'s truck he'd been leaning on and made a slight
hand gesture that brought the border collie to his side. He gave
J.J. a long, sideways look, squinting against the sun. "Sam
Malone always took good care of my mom, my sister and me.
Put both of us kids through school—just like he did Rachel,
you know? I know my mom will always have a home here,
and me—I don't need anything I haven't already got. So...
think what you want, Sheriff Fox." He took a few unhurried
steps, then turned back.

"Oh—feel free to use the computer in the study—we have
the internet, if you need to keep tabs on...things. You don't
need a password, nothing like that. Use the pool if you want—
it's down below on the other side of the house. Let me know
if you want to use the horses, or if you need anything. Just...
make yourselves at home. Or, you can go back to your life, if
you need to." He jerked his head toward the house. "She and
the baby, you know, they're safe here."

"Yeah, sure. Thanks." J.J. stayed where he was and thoughtfully watched the man and his dog go walking off down the
long curving drive between those stands of sentinel poplars
and evergreens, leaving in the same unhurried and confident
way they'd arrived.

Interesting guy. Although there was still something about
the man he wasn't sure he ought to trust. Definitely more going
on there than met the eye. *Well, time will tell,* he thought.
Meanwhile, he wasn't going anywhere.

He bent down and picked up his duffel bag and the car
seat/baby carrier and started up the flagstone steps. He made
it about halfway to the front door before it hit him. Hit him
like a fist to the belly. Hit him so hard he had to stop and set
the bag and carrier down and bend over to catch his breath.

*Put both of us kids through school—just like he did
Rachel...*

Questions hurtled dizzily through his mind: *Did Sam*

Malone pay for Rachel's education? If he did, why didn't she mention it? Does she even know?

One thing he knew for sure: if Sam Malone *had* funded Rachel's education, it changed everything. Rachel had said there wasn't anything connecting her with her grandfather, Sam Malone, but that wasn't true. Because money left a trail—a trail not of breadcrumbs, but pebbles, so easy a child could follow it.

Let alone the likes of Carlos Delacorte.

He had to tell her about this. Ask her if she knew. That's what he told himself as he picked up the carrier and bag and fumbled his way through the front door and into the house—that he needed to talk to Rachel about this new development. But the truth was, he just felt a powerful need to see with his own eyes that she was safe, even though he knew perfectly well she was, at least for the moment.

Or maybe he just felt a need *see* her. And he didn't stop, then, to ask himself *why*.

Inside, he found himself in a large foyer paved with Mexican terra-cotta tiles, which stretched across the width of the house to where double French doors opened onto a veranda. Beyond that he could see a sunlit courtyard filled with flowers, and hear the music from a large tiered fountain. Beyond the fountain, he could see Rachel sitting in a rocking chair, holding her baby. He couldn't see her clearly because she was in the shade of the veranda, but his heart stumbled anyway. Breath gusted from his chest, half relief, half consternation.

What the hell was that?

Before he could come up with a reasonable answer to that question, the housekeeper—Josie—entered the foyer through open double doors on his right.

"Oh—here you are," she exclaimed, smiling another one of her warm welcomes. "Come—I'll show you to your room. I…you know, I thought you'd want to be right next to Rachel's."

He nodded but didn't say anything, too shaken by his unanticipated response to seeing a woman he had no intimate connection to—if you didn't count delivering her baby and saving her life—to form coherent phrases.

He did recover enough to give Josie a smile to go with the nod, then followed her through the living room—a massive room with a high-vaulted and beamed ceiling that still managed to feel cozy, thanks to warm colors and comfortable furniture arranged in small, intimate groups—and a formal Spanish-style dining room with a table roughly the size of a tennis court. Beyond that was the kitchen, which appeared capable of providing food for a decent-sized restaurant, with all the modern conveniences he could think of and some he didn't even know the use for. All three rooms had big windows that looked out across manzanita and juniper and rock-studded hillsides to the green valley far below and the blue and purple mountains beyond. Impressive view, he thought. Not so great from a security standpoint.

He felt better, though, when Josie led him through a door off the kitchen and into what was obviously a bedroom wing. Here a wide hallway ran along the outside wall the entire length of the house. From it, doors opened into rooms which in turn opened onto the veranda and center courtyard. There were no doors in the outer wall, and the only windows were small and high. Except for the "public" wing, the house was built like a fortress.

"I hope this is okay—there are two more bedrooms on this side, and four more across the courtyard." Josie was standing in an open doorway, smiling at him.

He moved past her and into the room—a nice room, he noted; spacious, comfortable, clean—what else would he have expected? "This is fine." He could see Rachel through the French doors, sitting in a rocker, nursing her baby. He took a breath and felt himself relax a little. He glanced at the housekeeper. "Mind if I ask, where would Sam Malone's quarters be?"

"Oh—Sam—Mr. Malone's suite is down at the far end—next to the chapel." Was it his imagination, or did her cheeks seem pinker?

"Would you like something to drink?" Josie asked, one hand on the doorknob. "Coffee?"

"That would be great," he said absently as he set his duffel bag on the floor and walked toward the double French doors. Beyond them, he could see Rachel, her face turned away from him as she gazed at the baby nursing at her breast. Her hair hung loose over her shoulders like a shawl woven of black ink. Behind him he heard Josie's soft affirmation, then the door closing. He hesitated for a moment, then opened the doors and stepped out onto the veranda.

She turned her face toward him without surprise or alarm. Her eyes were heavy-lidded, her smile sleepy…sexy… sweet.

It had been a long time since he'd felt the emotion that flooded him then, but not so long he had trouble recognizing it for what it was.

Happiness.

Well, hell, he thought.

Hey, you're a cop—homicide. Tough guy. Who knew you'd be such a sucker for a broad with a baby?

Look, so you're attracted to her. She's drop-dead gorgeous—who wouldn't be? Get over it. What matters is what you're planning to do about it. Right?

Right. Which is nothing.

For all kinds of reasons. One, she just had a baby. Two, she just lost her husband. And three, she's a potential witness to a double murder in your protective custody, and the one who's going to save your miserable career.

So...hands off, Jethro.

"Hey," he said, his smile safely professional, "I see you and the little guy are settling in."

"Yes." She glanced down at the baby, and when she lifted her eyes to him again, he saw they were misty with tears.

He ran over in his mind all the reasons he'd just given himself to stay detached and braced himself.

"Thank you, Jethro," she said in a soft, choked voice.

He jerked back a little bit and said, "What for?"

"For bringing me here. I don't care what happens with my grandfather. I just...I feel safe here. You don't know how much that means to me."

Impassively, he watched a tear quiver on the edge of her lower lashes, then spill over and run down her cheek. "Hey, I'm glad you're happy," he said. "Just keep this little guy happy, too." He reached out and tweaked the blanket in the general vicinity of the baby's feet. Then he turned and went back into his room and closed the doors, closed his eyes and let out the breath he'd been holding.

No way in hell was he going to spoil it all for her by telling her how safe she *wasn't*.

From the memoirs of Sierra Sam Malone:

I never expected I'd be a father. For one thing, I never thought I'd be any good at it, given the kind of fatherhood I'd experienced firsthand growing up, and didn't care to pass that misery along to another poor helpless mite. But Elizabeth, she had other ideas. Evidently, she saw something in me the rest of the world had missed, because one day there I was, sitting beside her and holding on to her hand while she screamed and hollered and the doctor who'd come out from Barstow help her to bring our son, Sean, into the world.

Now, it wasn't a common thing in those days for the prospective father to be anywhere near where the action was. Most likely he'd be sent off to boil water or pace up and down and smoke cigarettes somewhere within earshot of the blood-curdling screams of his beloved so he'd know what a lousy good-for-nothing bastard he was for getting her into that state. Which would have been fine with me. But once again, Elizabeth, she had other ideas. Flat told me if I ran out on her then, once she got back on her feet she'd hunt me down like a mangy coyote and shoot me dead. And, I had good reason to believe she would.

So, that's why I was sitting there with her when the doc held up the squalling purple thing we'd agreed to call Sean Ronan Malone—after her father, not mine. And I have to tell you, I wasn't too impressed with him right off the bat. But then the doc, he laid that baby on Elizabeth's chest, all angry and wet and kicking and waving his fists like he was mad at the world. Laid him right on her...well, on her bare skin. And I have never forgotten—and I've had plenty of time to forget, since I've lived longer than I ever thought I would—never forgotten the way she looked as she gathered that baby in, the way she seemed to know just how to nestle him up against her breast, the way she looked at him, like he was all the world's treasure right there in her arms, the way she sang to him, half laughing, half crying, making a sound like a dove makes when she calls to her mate.

I thought then, and I still think, that was one of the most beautiful sights I or any man will ever see in this world.

He sat with the pen in his hand, trying to think of something else to write. After a minute or two, he gave it up, figuring maybe there wasn't anything else he had to say about that.

He laid the pen down on his desktop and picked up the cell phone that was lying there. He didn't much care for the damn thing, never had really got the hang of using it, but Sage had bought it for him and made him promise to carry it with him *at all times,* and had programmed it so all he had to do was push two buttons—one to turn it on and the other to call Sage. He had to admit it came in handy now and again.

He pushed the two buttons now, and Sage answered on the second ring, the way he always did, even though it was the middle of the night. He told the kid what he wanted, then tucked the phone in his shirt pocket and picked up his hat and put it on. He left the room, locked the door behind him, then took the chair lift down the spiral staircase to the ground floor. He was still perfectly capable of making it up and down those stairs on his own steam, but like the cell phone he put up with it because Sage had got it for him and Sage wanted him to use it. And…to be perfectly honest, the kid had a good practical head on his shoulders, and he did have a point. Which was that the old knees—maybe the hips, too—weren't as dependable as they used to be, and the last thing he wanted was to end his days laid up in a hospital bed or some rest home somewhere. He planned to go out swinging, if he possibly could.

Outside, the moon was bright enough for him to see his way, so he went carefully down the flagstone steps to wait in the lane for Sage. He could hear the soft clip-clop of hoof beats long before the horse and rider emerged from the shaded part of the drive, and as he watched the kid and his favorite painted horse come into the moonlight, he was thinking back to his Hollywood days. Thinking it was too bad Sage had been born too late for those old Westerns, because he'd have made one-helluva fine looking Indian.

Of course, they'd used white guys to play the Indians, back then, instead of real ones, which he'd always thought was a damn shame.

Sage pulled the paint up beside him and got off in the way he had of making it look a whole lot easier than it was. The paint whickered softly and bumped Sage with her head, and he scratched her under her jaw and slapped her on the neck, then turned to help him into the saddle—help he wasn't too proud to accept.

"You going to tell me where you're going?" Sage asked, once he'd got him settled.

"Thought I'd go up to the cabin for a while."

"Aren't you going to stick around to meet your grand-daughter?" The kid's voice wasn't accusing, just curious.

"Naw...thought I'd wait till they all get here. Get it all over with at once." He could see the kid turn his head to hide a grin, but didn't call him on it. After a moment he said, "What do you make of the fellow came with her?"

"The sheriff?" Sage shrugged his shoulders. "I don't know. Too soon to tell, maybe. But I like the look of the man."

He thought that over. Then he nodded. "So do I. I think he'll do right by her and the baby."

"Yeah," said Sage, "that's what I think, too."

He picked up the reins and clicked his tongue to the paint.

Sage said, "Need a light?"

"What for? Moon's high and bright and the horse knows the way." He leaned forward and the paint picked up the cue and broke into an easy lope. The horse's rhythms moved into his body and the years fell away and he was a young man again, riding with the night wind in his face and nothing but stars for company.

"I heard a horse last night," Rachel said to Josie as the housekeeper came through the doorway with a breakfast tray.

They were being served on a small flagstone patio off the

kitchen, warm and golden where the sun hit it first thing in the morning. J.J. watched the housekeeper unload the tray's contents onto the wrought-iron tabletop—bowls full of cereal and strawberries and a big glass of milk for Rachel; black coffee for him. Josie gave him a nervous smile and waited as he picked up his steaming mug and took a sip. He nodded his approval, then turned and strolled away toward the low wall that bordered the patio, providing an inviting front-row seat for that incredible view.

It was one of those times he wouldn't mind being a smoker, he thought. It'd give him an excuse to wander off by himself. He felt the need to do that—restless, uneasy.

He heard a faint clank as Rachel laid the baby monitor—another one of Katie's ideas—on the table.

"It sounded like it was right outside the house."

"Oh—that was probably Sage. Sometimes he likes to ride at night when the moon is bright."

The woman's words were reasonable enough, but there was something in her voice—a certain breathlessness—that made J.J.'s spine stiffen and his breathing go quiet. She's a lousy liar, too, he thought.

"Oh," Rachel said, stretching the word with a sigh, "it sounds wonderful."

"You like to ride?" Now Josie's voice was bright and eager.

"I love to ride. But it's been a long time…"

Suddenly he wasn't wishing he could find an excuse to leave. He made himself comfortable on the low wall, half turned so he could watch Rachel without seeming to while he sipped his coffee.

He'd already noticed the fact that she'd pulled her hair up in a high ponytail, then braided it so that it hung thick and glossy to brush the top bumps of her spine. And that she was wearing one of the outfits Katie had helped her pick out—loose-fitting top long enough to hang over the elastic waistband of the blue denim pants, for easy nursing and comfort while she was getting her figure back, according to Katie, who he figured ought to know.

Now, smiling, with pink in her cheeks and her bruises fading, Rachel looked both sweet and exotic…and a stranger to him.

He found himself flashing back to the woman he'd held in his arms not so long ago—vulnerable, sweaty and scared, not just a memory but a full sensory recall, the smell of her hair, salty with that hint of sweet flowers…the dampness of it against his cheek…the salty taste of it. The wiry strength of her body, and the way she'd trembled in spite of it. And he felt a twinge of something like sorrow…like loss. Hated himself for it, for wishing that traumatized girl back, but he couldn't deny the fact that he missed her. Then, touching her, holding her—it had seemed so natural. Now, to take her in his arms, kiss her—even chastely on her forehead, though God knew he'd rather taste her mouth instead, and not at all chastely—seemed all but unthinkable.

What are you thinking? She's a widow—husband hasn't been dead six months. She's just given birth, been beaten up, been through God only knows what kind of trauma. You're a sick man, Jethro.

"You're more than welcome to ride," Josie said, propping the empty tray against one hip. "Maybe not now—when you're ready. You just tell Sage—he'll fix you right up." She looked over at J.J. and smiled. "You, too—you're both welcome to use the horses, any time."

She went back into the house, and J.J. strolled over to the table, still sipping his coffee. He stood, casting a shadow across her sunny yellow blouse and pink cheeks, and said in a low growl, "Are you nuts? You can't go horseback riding. You just had a baby."

He could actually see her puff up, as if her body had suddenly grown quills all over, like a porcupine. Which didn't surprise him. He even wondered if he was trying to pick a fight with her on purpose.

"Give me some credit for knowing my own body," she said in a cold, clipped voice. She jerked back her head and aimed a brilliant black look at him. "I think *I'll* know when I feel up to going for a ride."

"Yeah?" He felt like a jerk, remembering belatedly that she'd been held a virtual prisoner for the past several months, so it was no surprise she wouldn't take well to being told what to do. Throttling back to a conversational tone, he asked, "Where'd you learn how to ride? Don't tell me Carlos keeps a stable."

She tossed her head so the braided ponytail took on a life of its own. "No, actually, my grandmother taught me. She loved horses, loved to go riding. I started riding lessons when I was about five. In fact, I could ride before I could speak English. We used to go almost every weekend, in Griffith Park. She had friends out in—" She broke off, shaking her head, and when she picked up her glass of milk and drank, he thought he caught the sheen of tears in her eyes.

He pulled out a chair and the wrought iron made a loud screechy sound on the flagstones. He cleared his throat as he put his coffee cup down and sat. "Well," he said, trying for a reasonable—not bossy—tone, "you can't go alone."

There was a long pause. Rachel set her milk glass down, licked milk from her lips and wiped the mustache that was left behind with the back of her hand. Watching her, his mouth watered as though he were beholding a banquet table.

Her eyes came up to meet his. "So," she said, unsmiling, "come with me."

Oh, hell. J.J. muttered something even he couldn't make out and sat back in his chair, shaking his head.

Her eyes took on a gleam. "What, don't tell me you don't know how to ride."

"I've ridden. Sure I have. I was on a horse—" He gave up trying to hold on to his masculine pride and let out a breath and with it a huff of laughter. "Once—when I was about six. Never again."

"Why not? What happened?" Her head tilted, eyes bright and curious.

He shrugged. Confession of his childhood humiliations didn't extend that far.

"You fell off? Hey, it happens. You're just supposed to get right back on."

His smile slipped sideways. "Ah, well…we weren't the ridin' kind of family, I guess."

"I'm sorry." She said it softly, as if he'd confessed to having some tragic illness. Then sighed and picked up her glass of milk. "Damn. There goes my John Wayne fantasy."

He snorted, and her eyes slid toward him, hooded and unreadable. Then, lashes lowered, she murmured, "Well, that's okay. Sage can go with me."

"Absolutely not."

"Why not?" Her eyes were wide open again, innocent as a babe's.

For the life of him, he couldn't come up with a reasonable answer. For one thing, he couldn't very well tell her he was envisioning some wild action movie scenario wherein a helicopter hovers over the meadow where Rachel is cantering in slow-mo through the wildflowers, and black-garbed ninja-types stream down the ladders, snatch her up and fly away.

Maybe he couldn't tell her why, but he knew he didn't want to let her out of his sight.

He said, "If anybody goes with you, it's going to be me."

Now demurely nibbling a strawberry, Rachel said, "Jethro, if I didn't know better, I'd say you sounded jealous."

He made a growling sound deep in his throat, shoved back his chair and got up and went back in the house. High time he got out of there, he thought, because he obviously needed to get his emotions and his fantasies under control. First, because there was this crazy question that insisted on flashing through his mind: *Is she flirting with me?* Which he *knew* was ridiculous, and nothing more than some wishful thinking on his part.

Then, there was the fact that she was right—he was behaving like a jealous man. And he simply was not the jealous type. Never had been, never would be.

Except…there was this voice arguing, way down deep inside his head: *Maybe you just never met a woman you thought was worth being jealous about.*

He just knew he couldn't stomach the thought of Rachel going riding with that kid, Sage. Or, the thought of the two of them galloping through the meadow full of wildflowers, matching black braids bouncing and blowing in the wind.

Chapter 9

Rachel waited for the sound of the door closing before she let out a slow and careful breath. Her heart was beating fast. She felt exhilarated. Excited. Even a little bit defiant. Why? Because she'd more than held her own against Sheriff Jethro J. Fox, even—*be truthful, Rachel*—flirted a little? And it had felt good?

Oh, how good it felt!

I'm happy, she thought. *I could…I wish I could…stay here.*

Of course, there was still the small matter of her grandfather to deal with, and why she'd been summoned, and what sort of inheritance she was supposed to claim and whether the man was alive or dead, for that matter. No one seemed to want to give her a definite answer to that question.

But she *was* happy, maybe just to feel safe. And free. Free to go for a walk, if she wanted to. As much as she hated to admit it, J.J. was right about the fact that her body probably wasn't ready to tolerate an activity like horseback riding, but he couldn't object to a walk. Even in hospitals, she thought, they encourage patients—which she certainly was not!—to *walk*.

She finished off the glass of milk, and then, after peeking down the front of her blouse to make sure the absorbent pads inside her nursing bra were in place, scooped up the baby monitor and went into the house to find Josie.

She found her in the kitchen cleaning up the breakfast dishes, and felt a jolt of shame as she realized she could easily have brought her own dishes in with her, saving the housekeeper the trip out to get them. *I'm sorry, Gran, I know you taught me better. I've gotten spoiled, living with Nicholas Delacorte these past three years. I'll do better.*

But Josie would have no part of her apology, and in fact even before Rachel could ask, offered to keep the baby monitor so Rachel could go for a walk.

"Oh, would you? Are you sure you wouldn't mind?" And just like that, those crazy hormone-fed emotions were flooding her again—fear at the thought of leaving her baby, yearning to get out in the morning if only for an hour, gratitude toward Josie for making it possible. She touched away a tear, then laughed at it and cleared her throat. "I, um…I just fed him—he's sleeping. He should be okay for an hour. I just want to… go out…to see—"

Josie hugged her, laughing. "Of course, he'll be okay, and no, I don't mind. I'll be right down there making beds anyway. You go on—take your time. Enjoy this beautiful morning."

Rachel laughed, too, and wiped away what remained of the tears. She put the baby monitor on the kitchen countertop, turned to give Josie another hug, then almost danced out of the kitchen, through the cavernous dining room, cozy living room and out the front door. She paused for a moment at the top of the flagstone steps to consider how Josie would call her if she needed her when she still didn't have a cell phone. She really did need to ask J.J. about getting one.

The thought flashed through her mind—just a hint of a thought—that maybe she should have a phone in case *she* needed to call for help, too. She dismissed it, partly because the idea of needing help, the thought of Carlos and his thugs being able to get to her here in this lovely place seemed so remote, and partly because J.J. was being so ridiculously paranoid and overprotective. She'd been paranoid herself for such a long time, and now that she was free, she was definitely *not* going to allow anyone to smother her, ever again.

She started off down the lane, and was both startled and a little uneasy, at first, when Moonshine hauled herself up out of the bed she'd made for herself in the shade of the evergreen trees and came to amble along at her heels. Then she decided it was kind of sweet, the notion of having a dog to protect her—not at all suffocating, as it would probably have been if J.J. had insisted on coming along.

"Okay," she told the dog, "you can come—as long as you don't tell J.J. on me. Deal?" And she was surprised and oddly touched when the dog shuffled up beside her and bumped her head under her hand, as if she'd understood. As she obliged the dog with a pat on her wrinkled forehead, she laughed a little at the peculiar sensation she felt in the vicinity of her heart. Maybe, she decided, dogs weren't so bad after all.

She made her way quickly through the maze of flower and rose beds, emerging onto the stretch of the lane that ran along the meadow. She paused at the barbed wire fence to watch the horses grazing in the new spring grass, then decided there was no reason she couldn't go into the meadow and see the horses up close.

She soon discovered that getting through a barbed wire fence was trickier than it looked, and was very glad she hadn't had to do it for the first time in front of witnesses. Particularly Sheriff J. J. Fox.

"You," she said to Moonshine, who was sitting on her

haunches in the meadow grass, watching her with tongue hanging out, "had better not be laughing." Moonshine made no comment.

Flushed and exhilarated, Rachel dusted her hands and set out toward the horses, who by now had seen her and, being curious, as all horses are, were coming to see who this newcomer was. In moments, to her utter delight, she was surrounded by the four mares and two geldings. Most were bay or dark chestnut, but for one dappled gray and a beautiful black with appaloosa spots on her rump.

Unlike dogs, horses held absolutely no fear for her, which she supposed was odd, considering their size and the fact that they were more than capable of doing her harm if they wanted to. But she'd always felt completely at home with horses—loved their warmth and their smell and the ways they had of talking with their ears and eyes and the way they held their heads. And these seemed to accept her instantly as a friend, whickering softly and reaching toward her with their velvety muzzles, jostling for the privilege of being the closest and the first to be petted. One even bumped Rachel's back with her head, which made her laugh with sheer joy.

"Oh," she lamented aloud, "I wish I'd brought you some treats. I'm sorry—I'll bring some next time, okay?"

After crooning to them and stroking and petting each in turn, she said a reluctant goodbye to the horses and slipped between their big warm bodies to continue her walk across the meadow. The horses followed a few paces, whickering in disappointment, then stopped to watch her make her way down a slope toward a thicket of willows and cottonwoods that bordered the far side of the meadow.

There was a creek there, she discovered, and just beyond the creek and the trees, brush and boulder-covered hills rose to meet taller mountains thick with junipers and bull pines. The creek was running too high at this time of year to risk crossing, but she found a nice rock in the shade at the water's edge, sat on it and began to take off her shoes. Moonshine, who had been off rambling through the meadow grass in pursuit of her own pleasures, came to flop down in the cool sand a short distance away, panting happily.

The ice-cold water on her bare feet made Rachel gasp, at first. Then laugh out loud. She wiggled her toes in the clear water and giggled as minnows darted away from the alien intrusion.

"Feels good, don't it?"

She ducked instinctively and jerked her feet out of the water, heartbeat gone wild on adrenaline. Still in a half crouch, she cautiously lifted her head to search for the source of the voice.

On the other side of the creek, an old man was sitting on a paint horse, leaning on the saddle horn, watching her. A chill ran through her, one that had nothing to do with the ice water running past her bare toes, as she realized she hadn't heard him approach, probably because of the noise the creek made. Anybody could have sneaked up on her. *Anybody.*

In the time it took to draw two good breaths, she sized him up: *Old, but still looks fairly fit, especially sitting up there on that horse. Big, but he looks like he used to be bigger. Age has shrunk him.*

And this one really does look like John Wayne.

He wore a cowboy hat and a leather vest hanging open over blue denim shirt and jeans. His hair was gray—almost white—and hung well over his collar. He hadn't shaved in a while.

"I'm not trespassing," she said.

The old man threw back his head and laughed out loud.

Annoyed rather than reassured, Rachel straightened and let her feet drop back into the water. "Why is that funny?"

"It isn't," the old man drawled in a cracking voice. "You just reminded me of somebody I used to know." He leaned across the saddle horn and nodded with his head in the direction she'd come from. "You'd be from up at the big house, I expect. Kin to old Sam Malone."

Her heart had accelerated again, but she tried to keep any traces of eagerness out of her voice. "Do you—did you—know him?"

The old man scratched his chin whiskers and considered. "Yep. Sure. Used to know him well. 'Course, that was before he turned into a crazy old cuss."

Rachel said dryly, "Childhood friend, huh?" The old man gave another bark of laughter.

"That your dog?" He nodded toward Moonshine, who was still lounging in the shade, seemingly unconcerned by the stranger's sudden appearance.

"No, she belongs to a…friend." *Some watchdog you are,* she thought.

"Used to have a dog like that. Long time ago—when I was a kid." He sounded regretful, and his eyes had gone faraway and sad.

Feeling an obscure desire to cheer him, Rachel said, blatantly teasing, "Couldn't have been all that long ago, then."

The old man reared back and glared fiercely down at her from his high saddle. "Young woman, are you flirting with me?"

She smiled, not at all intimidated. "Yes, I believe I am."

He snorted. "Why, I'm old enough to be your grandpa."

Rachel sighed. "I kind of wish you were. I mean, instead of the 'crazy old cuss' who *is* my grandfather."

His eyes narrowed, and even with the whiskers and the width of the creek between them she could see a smile play around the corners of his mouth. "Now, missy, why would you say a thing like that? You don't know me from Adam."

She lifted her head to look at him, shaking her braid back over her shoulder. "I don't—didn't know him, either," she said evenly. "But I know he hurt someone I love dearly."

There was a pause, then the old man nodded and looked away. "I can believe that. Yep…I can believe that." After a moment he sighed and his head swiveled back to her. "What makes you think I haven't hurt my share of good people in my lifetime, too?"

She leaned back on her hands and regarded him, thinking about it. "I don't know…you just don't seem like you would. Not on purpose, anyway."

He made a sound—a bark of laughter. "Not now, maybe. But, listen, I was a different person in my younger days. Maybe you wouldn't have thought so well of me if you'd known me back then."

"Maybe not," she said, and stubbornly added, "but then again, maybe I would."

She was surprised when he laughed again, that deep in the belly, head thrown back guffaw that made him seem years younger than she knew he probably was. "You sure do remind me of someone I used to know."

"Yeah? Who's that?"

"Missy," he said, leaning across the saddle horn, squinting at her with one eye, "I don't know you well enough to tell you that."

"You know," she retorted, "you remind me of someone, too." And she had to smile.

"Yeah? Who's that?" Mocking her.

Her smile broadened; laughter tickled beneath her breastbone. "John Wayne."

The old man laughed again—not a guffaw but a different kind of laugh and it faded quickly. Somberly, he said, "The Duke was a helluva man. I was—I'd a' been proud to stand in his shadow."

Before Rachel could respond to that, they both heard a distant whistle. Moonshine lurched to attention, staring back up the slope toward the ranch house.

"Yeah," the old man drawled, nodding in the same direction, "that'll be your 'friend,' I expect. Looking for his dog." His eyes slid sideways, coming back to rest on Rachel. "Or, maybe it's you he's lookin' for."

She muttered a denial under her breath, and he smiled, showing strong, even teeth among the whiskers. "You know, missy, there's worse things than a man who thinks enough of a woman to want to keep her safe."

He touched a finger to his hat brim and went riding off, quickly disappearing behind the thicket of willows and cottonwoods.

Rachel stuffed her feet into her shoes and slid off the rock, discovering only then how oddly quivery she felt inside. More unsettled by her unexpected visitor than she realized, evidently. Something nagged at her, but J.J. was coming, and for the life of her, she couldn't think what it was....

As she climbed up the steeper slope of the creek bed, she could see him making his way across the meadow, and Moonshine trotting out to meet him. The horses had moved away down to the far end of the meadow. Her steps slowed, then stopped, without her being aware of telling them to, and as she stood watching the tall figure of the sheriff come toward her, she realized she wasn't angry with him for coming to find her, or even mildly annoyed. What she felt instead, she was almost sure, was *pleasure*. She put one hand over her mouth to hide a smile as J.J. stepped carefully around something—a pile of cow or horse manure—and pressed the other against the spreading warmth in her still spongy middle, and thought about what the old man said about a man who thinks enough of a woman to want to keep her safe.

Did Nicky? About me? I honestly don't know....

But…honestly? She was pretty sure Nicky hadn't thought much about anyone but himself.

I'm not going to say anything to make her mad.

That had been the thought uppermost in J.J.'s mind as he picked his way through the minefield of cow pies and horse apples. He was determined not to scold her for going out alone, after he'd expressly told her not to. He kept reminding himself she was a grown woman, and just because she was his witness—potentially—didn't give him the right to treat her like his prisoner. Or a child.

Not that he thought of her that way. Far from it. He paused, with Moonshine panting juicily at his side, and watched her come closer, and he thought he'd never seen anyone look less childlike. In spite of her small stature, she seemed to him the very picture of womanhood—cheeks pink and eyes bright, the sun striking fire in her shiny dark hair…figure lush and full beneath the loose-fitting top she wore, molded to her body now by the breeze.

He waited for her to get close enough, then told her, with an unexpected gruffness in his voice, "I've got some news about your friend. Thought you'd want to know."

She halted, and a look he was familiar with flashed across her face. *Guilt.* She'd forgotten all about her friend Izzy, he could see that. At least for a moment.

Concern instantly replaced the guilt. "Is she—"

"She's fine. Evidently you were right about Carlos, at least as far as his feelings about harming nuns go. She's back working at her clinic, none the worse for wear."

"Her car—"

"I've made arrangements for it to be returned to her."

She closed her eyes, put a hand to her forehead and breathed a fervent, "Thank you."

Then there was a moment…a silent, awkward moment…

while she simply gazed at him, lips slightly parted, as if there was something more she wanted to say. A suspenseful moment, when it almost seemed to J.J. she was leaning toward him. Then she reached up and touched his face.

He jerked back, and a breath he didn't know he'd been holding came gusting from his chest.

"Oh. Sorry—" She pressed her fingertips to her lips but they failed to hide the smile that had formed there. "You, um…you had…there was some toilet paper. A little bit. Right *there*. I guess you cut yourself shaving. Again."

"Oh—yeah." He laughed without humor, touching the spot that still felt the imprint of her fingers.

"You do that a lot, I've noticed." He could see the hint of a dimple in her cheek as she turned to begin strolling back toward the house.

He fell in beside her, and Moonshine hauled herself out of the grass and padded along behind. "Yeah…" he drawled, "guess I'm kind of out of practice doing that kind of thing. Shaving."

She threw him a look. "How come?"

He snorted, thinking how dumb his little rebellion seemed now. "Not important." He walked a bit, then tossed away a grass stem he'd been fiddling with. He felt compelled to add, "Might not believe it now, but used to be…back when I was on the detective squad…I could clean up pretty good. You know—military haircut, suit and tie…the works."

She turned to give him another look, a longer one, this time, shading her eyes with one hand against the morning sun. A measuring look, he thought, and felt a curious stirring low in his body.

"Did you like doing that?"

He hadn't expected that particular question, and had to think about it. After a moment he shrugged and said, "It went with the job. And I did like doing *that*."

She didn't say anything for several steps. Then, without looking at him: "Do you really hate it so much? Being out here, I mean?"

"Out 'here'?" He waved a hand and managed a smile of sorts. "You mean, out *there*—in the freakin' *desert?* What's not to hate?"

She glanced at him, then looked away quickly, and he realized that for some reason his answer was important to her. And without fully understanding why, he found he really wanted to give her an honest answer, if he could. So he thought about it for a while. Then he said slowly, "Okay…maybe there are some things—one or two—I'd keep. Old Moonshine, there, being one. But…thing is, I liked putting killers behind bars." A knot had formed in his chest, and he had to clench his teeth and use some force to push words past it. "I *really* did like doing that. And out here—" He hitched in a breath, forced another smile he didn't feel. "Anyway, I really want to get back to that, someday."

And you're the one who's going to help me do that. God willing and I play my cards right.

He was going to have to tell her that, soon, and start asking the questions that would change everything between them. Questions that would put him firmly on one side of the law and order divide, and her on the other. But he couldn't bring himself to do it just then. Not yet, he told himself, without knowing why he dreaded it so. *Not yet.*

He noticed she'd gone quiet, and that the brightness and smiles had gone away. He wondered if she'd somehow picked up on the guilt he was feeling, which naturally made him feel that much guiltier. He tried to think of something he could say, something they could talk about, something…ordinary. Like… small talk. But he couldn't think of a thing, and it occurred to him that maybe somehow their relationship had bypassed the small talk stage. He didn't know if that was a good thing, or a bad one.

They'd almost reached the fence when she hitched in a breath, like a preamble to something momentous, and then came out with, "I saw a man, just now. Down by the creek."

He halted in his tracks. "What? What do you mean, you saw a man? Who was he? Why didn't you tell me this?"

She let out the breath in an impatient gust. "Because I knew you'd do this—overreact. And he was harmless—just an old guy on a horse."

"So, why are you telling me this now?"

"Because I thought I should. Look, don't make a big deal out of it. I was resting by the creek, and he stopped to say hello. I think he must be a neighbor—he said he knew my— knew Sam Malone."

"Neighbor?" J.J. waved his arm in a wide arc. "Do you see any neighbors around here?" He paused, fighting for calm. "Okay. You said he was on a *horse?* Did he give you his name?"

Uncertainty crossed her face. "Well, no, I didn't…"

He swore under his breath. "What did he look like?"

"Um…don't laugh, okay?" He didn't tell her laughing was the furthest thing from his mind; he figured she already knew that. In stony silence he watched her bite her lower lip, watched a smile duel with a grimace. "He looked like John Wayne."

He smacked a hand to his forehead. "Oh, for—"

"Except old," she added quickly. "Longish whitish hair… beard… But, he was nice, I swear. Quite a character." She paused and added with a touch of defiance, "I *liked* him."

He folded his arms on his chest and looked at her, and she looked right back at him, not budging an inch. And it took about ten seconds of that before he realized he wasn't as annoyed with her as he should have been, and that what he wanted to do more than anything was haul her in and kiss her right where she stood.

"Well, okay—this time," he said finally, on an exhalation of surrender, "but you need to take a cell phone with you when you go out from now on. Will you do that for me, at least?"

She let out a breath, too. "I was going to ask you about that. I need to get one."

"I'll take care of it."

"Okay…good."

Since it seemed they'd arrived at a truce of sorts, he turned to the fence and slipped easily between two strands of barbed wire. Then he put his foot on the middle strand and pulled up on the top one to make a space for Rachel to get through. She gave him a grateful look and stooped down to climb through the opening, but he could see she needed something to hold to steady her, so he just naturally gave her his free hand.

Hanging on to him, she managed to get halfway through the fence before she lost her balance. Then he had to let go of the top wire in order to grab her and keep her from falling, so of course then one of the barbs got caught in her hair. By the time he'd got her extricated from the fence and standing on her own two feet, he was sweaty and flustered and so was she. And somehow or other, she'd wound up pretty much in his arms.

For a long moment, neither of them seemed inclined to do anything about that, even though J.J. knew he ought to. That he *had* to. Because one thing he could not do was go on standing there with his arms around her and her body warm and damp and soft against him. Things would happen, then, he knew, that would make it next to impossible for him to ever put her on the other side of that law and order divide. So he mustered all his willpower and eased up his hold on her.

For a moment she stayed where she was, not moving away from him, just looking up at him, cheeks pink and lips parted, as if there was something urgent she had to say. Instead, suddenly she sucked in breath in a sharp gasp and pushed away, one hand on her blouse, right over her breasts. She glanced down at herself, then back at him, and backed away, looking like she wished she could be anyplace else but where she was.

"I'm sorry," he muttered, feeling like the world's biggest jerk. "I didn't mean—hey, it won't happen again. Okay? I don't want you to think—"

"Funny," she said, her voice soft and breathless, "I was just thinking how sweet you were to keep me from making a complete fool of myself."

She turned and walked quickly away from him, head down and ponytail slapping against her collar, leaving him as confused as he'd ever felt in his life.

One thing for sure. Before this gets any more complicated, I'm gonna have to find a way to ask her those questions.

Like, were you with your husband the night he was killed? Did you see who shot him?

And most importantly, what else *did you see?*

The baby was fussing.

Again?

Rachel groaned and peered at the clock radio on the nightstand. Big glowing digits proclaimed the time: Four o'clock. In the morning.

She rolled onto her side, and every part of her body felt as though it were made of lead. Even her hair felt heavy. Using all her willpower, she managed to sit up and swing her legs over the side of the bed, then stand upright. She shuffled the few short steps to the bassinet and stood for a moment looking down at her son. In the soft glow of the nightlight, she could see him squirming and waving his fists, his face scrunched up with eyes shut tight and mouth wide open, the very picture of infant displeasure.

"Hey, sweet boy," she crooned, and even though her throat ached, her voice was musical and soothing as a lullaby. "How can you be hungry again already? I just fed you an hour ago."

Inside, she was screaming, *I can't do this! I can't do it alone. Dammit, I wasn't supposed to have to do this alone.*

"What am I going to do with you, huh? I don't have any more milk, and I'm so sore—" Her voice broke. Whispering, "I'm sorry, I'm sorry…shh…" she scooped up her now-wailing son and cuddled him, joggling him and patting him, to no effect whatsoever.

She began to pace in utter despair, and then from somewhere in her sleep-fogged brain a memory surfaced: a nurse, at the hospital, giving her some bottles of formula…telling her she might need to supplement feedings until her milk came in, if the baby didn't seem to be getting enough.

Yes!

Okay, she thought, almost crying with relief, this would definitely seem to qualify as one of those times. The bottles— where were they? The kitchen, probably—Josie had helped her unpack, she'd most likely put them in the refrigerator.

She tucked the frantic baby into the crook of one arm, opened her bedroom door, peered out, then hurried down the empty corridor to the kitchen. The Mexican paving tiles were cold on her bare feet, but she didn't think about that, or the fact that she was only wearing underpants and the sweatshirt J.J. had given her to wear to bed her first night out of the hospital, the night she'd spent in his trailer.

In the kitchen, whimpering, "I'm sorry, I'm sorry…shh…" she opened the huge custom-built refrigerator and took out the six-pack of formula bottles. She set it on the tiled top of the large island in the middle of the kitchen that served as both work space and casual eating area. Now what? How was she supposed to get one bottle out using only one hand, while juggling a crying baby? She was trying her best to do that, trying not to succumb to sobs of exhaustion and frustration, when she felt a rush of warmth against her back, and hands heavy on her shoulders.

Chapter 10

"Here, here—let me have him."

J.J.'s voice sounded husky and cracked and rough as sandpaper, and oh-so-beautiful to her ears.

She uttered a sound that was somewhere between a laugh and a sob as she half turned toward him, and his hands slipped down her arms, so deft and sure she surrendered her baby to them without a moment's hesitation.

"Shh…" he murmured, crooning to the baby as he rocked him, with a rasping sound like a tiger's purr. And miraculously, her son stopped crying and opened his eyes and turned his face toward the sound.

Then, for a moment, she simply stood still, utterly captivated by the vision of her tiny newborn baby nestled against Sheriff Jethro J. Fox's broad chest. His *bare* chest, adorned only by a modest furring of golden brown hair that arrowed down the middle of his torso to disappear beneath the drawstring waistband of the sweatpants he wore, riding dangerously low on narrow hips.

"I'd hurry up with that," he drawled, glancing up at her and nodding toward the package of formula bottles now forgotten on the island top. "I've got his attention, but I don't know for how long."

"I'm so sorry. I didn't mean to wake you," she muttered as she fumbled with the package, at the same time trying to brush the tears from her cheeks without him noticing.

"*You* didn't," he said dryly, and his eyes were once more on the baby in his arms.

Which gave her a chance to look at him again, and she did—a longer look that took in the sheet-wrinkle across one cheekbone and the dark beard-shadow on the lower half of his face. Her heart did a curious flip-flop, and she had to look away.

She sniffed. "I'm sorry, I guess I don't have enough…um, to feed him. I've nursed him three times…" Tears threatened again, and she gazed blindly through them at the bottle in her hand.

"You gonna heat that up, or what?"

She cleared her throat…swiped at her cheek. "Um…it says you're not supposed to microwave it."

"How 'bout if you just run some hot water in a pan and set the bottle in it. That's what—couple ounces? Shouldn't take but a minute."

Rachel found a pan behind the second cupboard door she tried. She ran water in the sink until it was hot, filled the pan with it and set the formula bottle in the water, then turned and leaned her backside against the edge of the sink.

To her continued amazement, Sean was still staring intently at J.J.'s face, evidently entranced by the sight. So, she discovered, was she. Too much so.

She turned quickly back to the sink, picked up the bottle and swirled it. Silence thickened in the room while she tested the heat of the formula on her arm, swirled some more, tested again. Satisfied at last with the temperature—or unnerved by the silence—she carried the bottle over to where J.J. now sat, comfortably half reclining in a chair at the island, Sean tucked neatly in the curve of his arm.

"Okay—" breathless, she held out her arms "—I think it's okay now."

Instead of turning over her baby, J.J. made a hand gesture. *Give it to me.* So, she passed him the formula bottle. A moment later, with a tiny pang that felt oddly like jealousy, she watched her son gulp greedily at the nipple, making the same squeaky sounds he always made when he nursed. His dark eyes were still fastened on J.J.'s face.

"Where'd you get so good at this?" she whispered.

J.J. didn't answer right away. He'd noticed her legs were bare all the way up to the edge of his old "Life's a Beach" sweatshirt. Bare, smooth, pale golden skin that looked silky soft to the touch…muscles firm and well-defined…reminded him of a dancer's legs. It took some effort, but he managed to haul his attention away from the vision.

"My sister's got three," he said with a one-shouldered shrug, keeping his eyes on the baby where they belonged. "Last one came while her husband was in Afghanistan. I helped her out a time or two." He paused, then glanced up to meet her eyes and said with an unexpected harshness in his voice, "Nobody should have to do this by themselves."

"I didn't plan to." She looked away, and he could see her swallow—hard. "Nicky—" She stopped.

"Should have been here for you," he finished for her. "Yeah, I know. Should be your husband sitting here right now, instead of me."

She laughed, and he hadn't expected that, either. He stared at her. "What's funny about that?"

"It's not—except…I can't picture Nicholas doing…what you're doing." She paused, evidently thinking about it, and he could see she didn't feel like laughing anymore. She hitched a shoulder. "He probably would have hired a nanny."

J.J. snorted. "Hey, whatever works. I guess if you've got the money to hire help..."

She shook her head, and couldn't seem to look at him. "He wouldn't have wanted me to nurse, either."

"You didn't get a say in it?"

Looking at the floor, she said in a low voice, "It's just that—" she caught a breath "—he would have wanted me all to himself."

Nice guy, he thought, but said aloud, "Well, I guess he must have really loved you."

She lifted her head and shot him a defiant look. But before she looked away again he saw a tear-track glimmer on her cheek.

"What, you don't think he did?" She shook her head slightly, but didn't reply. He waited.

After a moment, she drew a breath that seemed to steady her, and said in a low voice, "I thought he did—obviously. Or else, why would I have married him? But lately, I've been... wondering about that."

"That being whether he loved you or why you married him?" It occurred to him that he was interrogating her, but either she hadn't realized it yet, or didn't mind.

"Both, actually. I thought he loved me...but now I think—I know he loved the way I looked—the way we looked together. He told me often enough—he thought I was beautiful."

Suspense sizzled inside him and raced beneath his skin. Was this the moment? They were on the subject. He could easily steer the conversation to that last night she'd spent with her husband. So easily...

She drew another of those bolstering breaths. "Now, what I think is, he loved the *idea* of me, but I don't think he ever really knew—never even *saw* the real me."

The moment had passed…like a river flowing past his feet.

He smiled and said, "And…who *is* the real you?"

He saw her lips quiver with the hint of an answering smile. "Well…let's just say…I'm no angel, okay?" She looked down, her face somber again. "I think the main thing is, I don't look like who I really am. I think I look…you know, little, and, um…kind of sweet—" she coughed and colored a little "—but actually, I have a temper, and I'm a lot tougher, a lot stronger than I look."

"I can testify to that," J.J. said, flashing back to those incredible moments with her in the backseat of his patrol vehicle. "I've seen what you can do, remember?" He glanced down at the baby now sleeping in his arms, then back at Rachel, and knew that she, too, remembered. Remembered the intimacies that hadn't bothered her at the time, but maybe were beginning to, judging from the way the pink in her cheeks was deepening.

The moment stretched while he tried his best to block those memories from his mind. Then he frowned, forced himself to concentrate on the present and said, "How do you know your husband wouldn't have loved 'the real you'? Did you ever let him see that side?"

She snorted softly. "I guess not."

"Why?"

She paused, restless now, and he could see the question made her uncomfortable. In a muffled voice, not looking at him, she said, "I was afraid, I suppose. Afraid he wouldn't want to marry me. Isn't that stupid? That I really did want to marry him, so badly."

"Which brings up the second question—why?"

Again, she didn't answer right away, and he saw another tear run down her cheek. She brushed at it, sniffed and muttered, "Sorry. I don't usually do this."

"That's okay," he said gruffly. "Hormones. My sister was a mess for weeks." He was rewarded with a small laugh.

She frowned at the moisture on her fingertips. "Yeah, well. This is very hard on my self-esteem, you know?" She took a breath, faced it head-on. "What I've been asking myself is, what kind of person does it make me, that I was so desperate to marry a man who was basically spoiled, selfish, immature and was probably going to make me miserable at some point in the future?"

J.J. just looked at her while he worked on getting his own emotions under control. Because inside him there was a guy doing the fist-pump and hissing, *Yes!* Which was hard to understand, since even if she *was* having doubts about whether she'd loved her husband and maybe wasn't as deeply mired in grief as he'd thought, it didn't change anything as far as those questions he needed to ask her went. Except as a potential eyewitness, she was still as far off-limits to him as ever, at least for the time being.

But...for the future? He couldn't keep the thought out of his head. Once he was back on the detective squad where he belonged and out of that desert purgatory...what then? How long did it take for a woman to get over the loss of her husband, even if he had been a selfish son of a bitch?

"Well," he said, "did you know any of that then?"

She sniffed and whispered, "No, I suppose not."

He cleared his throat and said carefully, "Let me ask you this. Nicholas Delacorte was a good-looking guy...right?"

"Oh, yes." She gave a husky laugh and brushed again at her cheek.

"Charming?"

She nodded. "Yes—very."

"And rich?"

"Yes, but that didn't—"

"He treated you well?"

"Like a queen." She'd gone still, and was staring at him intently now.

He shrugged, and forced the words out. They came, sounding like a truckload of gravel. "What's not to love? You were young, vulnerable, maybe a little rebellious, like you said—and he had a touch of danger about him, too, right?" She nodded slowly. He tipped his head toward her. "So, there you go. Don't beat yourself up about it."

He set the empty formula bottle on the island top and stood up. She took a step toward him. He strolled toward her with her sleeping baby a warm, sweet weight in his arms. Close enough to hand her son off to her, he paused, and for what seemed a long time, just stood and looked down at her. And for some reason, she looked back at him, and her lips parted. He felt her warmth, smelled her scent—baby powder and milk and woman—and dangerous thoughts and wants filled his head. *Not for you,* he reminded himself. *At least, not now.*

He made a throat-clearing sound and she seemed to echo it, and they performed an awkward little dance while he did his best to hand over the kid without waking him up.

"Might want to burp him before you put him down," he said gruffly, when his arms were empty again. He turned and hauled himself away from her, and it was like trying to break free of a magnetic field. The place on his body where the baby had nestled felt cold now.

At the kitchen doorway he paused to look back. Giving full credit to his vigilant Better Angel, who must have been perched on his shoulder just then, he cleared his throat and said, "Oh—you might think about giving your husband a break, too. Maybe the man loved you as much as he knew how to. Given the kind of upbringing he had."

Whether that was true or not, he didn't know. Maybe it would give her some comfort. Hell, he could do that for her, at least.

He went through the door and down the hallway to his room. To bed, but probably not to sleep.

"I saw her, yesterday. Down by the creek. Talked to her."

It was early morning. Sam was leaning against a stack of alfalfa hay, watching Sage milk.

The kid looked sideways at him without stopping the rhythmic *thrum-thrum* of milk into the foam-filled bucket. "Yeah? Funny she didn't mention meeting you."

"She didn't know it was me, and I didn't enlighten her."

"Why not?"

He laughed silently. "Well, I've been told I'm a coward."

"A coward?" Sage threw him another look, eyebrows raised. "Who told you that?"

"Doesn't matter." Sam moved restlessly. It was warm in the barn, but he didn't take off the fleece-lined jacket he wore. The older he got, he noticed, the harder it was to keep the old bones warm. "Truth is, I liked talking with her. Found out how she feels about me, too. Her not knowing who I was, she didn't mince words." He cackled a laugh. "Sure did remind me of her grandmother. Not her looks, of course. But she does have a way about her."

He watched Sage kick back the milking stool and stand up, envying the kid his thirty-year-old's agility. Waited while the kid carried the bucketful of milk to the milk room, poured it through the strainer, then into stainless steel cans. Watched him put the cans in the walk-in, then come back to release the cow from the stanchion, give her a slap on her bony rump to send her ambling back out to pasture. Pick up a push broom that was leaning against the wall, then finally come back to him.

"When you planning on telling her who you are?" Sam shrugged and didn't reply. Sage made a couple of passes with the broom, then paused to look at him. "Still planning to wait till they all get here? Tell everybody at the same time?"

Sam plucked an alfalfa stem from a bale of hay and chewed on it. "I don't know, I'm thinking of playing dead awhile longer. They think I'm already dead, maybe I'll find out how they really feel about me. Find out why they're really here."

Sage snorted. "You know why they're here."

"The money, you mean."

"That letter you sent said, come and claim your inheritance. You could have said, come and meet your grandpa, but you didn't. What did you expect them to do?"

Sam made a scoffing sound. "If I'd said come meet grandpa, you think they'd come? Only way I could be sure they'd show up was to offer money."

Sage gave him one of his inscrutable Indian looks. "Maybe. But now you're never gonna know, are you? You didn't give them a chance to show you whether or not they care about meeting you for *you*."

Damn kid, Sam thought. He hated it when Sage was right.

He shoved himself away from the haystack and picked up his hat. "So, that's why I'm gonna play dead," he muttered. "Give 'em the chance to say what they really think about old Sierra Sam Malone." He jammed the hat on his head, picked up the reins of his paint horse and made for the door.

"You going back up to the cabin?"

"Figure I better, if I'm playin' dead. Can't play the crotchety old neighbor too many more times. That little gal is no fool. And neither is that lawman she brought with her."

"No, they're not," Sage agreed. There was silence. Sam kept walking. Sage said, "You want a leg up on that horse, or not?"

Sam eyeballed the height of the stirrup, then reluctantly halted and waited, hands on the saddle horn, for Sage to come up beside him. "Damnation, I hate bein' *old*," he grumbled as he planted his boot in the cradle Sage made of his interlaced fingers.

"You rather die young?" Sage said, and lifted him effortlessly into the saddle.

The next morning, Sage took Rachel to show her the farm and the old original adobe farmhouse where he now lived. J.J. was all set to go with them when Katie called him on his cell phone with information he'd asked her to get for him and for which he knew he was going to need to refer to his computer. Since he couldn't think of a good reason to ask Sage and Rachel to wait for him, he had no choice but to wave them on without him.

It wasn't that he really thought Sage might present some kind of danger to his potential eyewitness, or that Carlos's thugs were lurking out there in the barn waiting to grab her. It was more of an indefinable uneasiness he felt—like an itch in a place he couldn't reach to scratch. An itch brought on by that image that kept drifting into his mind of the two of them, Sage and Rachel, galloping side by side on horseback, both with similar long black hair flowing in the wind....

Funny, he thought, how much those two looked alike. Like a matched set.

And none of his business, when he got right down to it. None whatsoever.

Back in the study, with the house quiet around him, J.J. squinted at the computer screen and picked up his cell phone.

"Okay, I've got it. Talk to me, Katie. What am I looking at, here?"

"Well, first of all, you were right, Sam Malone did pay for Rachel's college education, including medical school. Deposits had been made regularly to a trust fund set up by Rachel's grandmother, Elizabeth Doyle Malone. The trust fund itself has no connection to Sam Malone, but the deposits came from one of his more obscure holdings, a pharmaceutical company headquartered in Dublin, Ireland. Obscure, but easily traceable to Malone."

"What's the status of the trust fund now?"

"Inactive since the death of Elizabeth Malone, currently being administered by a law firm in Beverly Hills. Presumably, since the trust is supposed to be for the costs of Rachel's education, once she dropped out, the payments stopped. If she completes her education, then funds remaining in the trust are to be given to Rachel."

"Huh. Did Rachel know about the trust?"

"Who knows? It doesn't seem to be a big secret, but if she does know, based on what you told me about her attitude toward Grandpa, I'm guessing she thinks it was established and funded by her grandmother."

"So," J.J. said grimly, "if it's no big secret, anybody trying to figure out where a runaway eyewitness might go, anybody looking for family connections, say…"

"Could easily find out about the trust and who funded it," Katie finished for him.

He let out a breath, counted ten, then said, as he bookmarked the page and logged off, "Any developments in the case of the two dead federal agents?"

"Nothing I've been able to find. Also, no word on whether Carlos Delacorte is under surveillance."

J.J. snorted. "I think it's a pretty safe bet the feds have been watching the entire Delacorte organization for a while now. Which I'm thinking is probably what led to the attempted takedown outside that nightclub to begin with."

"Probably," said Katie, "but even if that's true, the feds aren't likely to be sharing their information with the San Bernardino County Sheriff's Department."

"Not with a lowly deputy from an armpit of a desert outpost

out in the middle of nowhere, anyway," J.J. said sourly. He let out another gust of frustration, thanked Katie for her efforts, told her to keep trying to get a line on Carlos's activities and signed off.

With the computer screen blank, the cell phone silent and Josie evidently occupied in some distant quarter, the house seemed silent as a tomb. Since there was still no sign of Rachel and Sage, J.J. figured he'd go to his room and get his hat, then maybe take a walk down to the farm…see if he could meet up with them. He started across the courtyard to his room, then at the last moment, found himself taking a slight detour to Rachel's room next door instead.

The French doors to both his and Rachel's rooms stood open onto the veranda. He paused there, taking in the sweet smells of flowers and the warm spring breeze, listening to the wind chimes and for sounds of infant displeasure. Hearing none, he hesitated, and then, with no idea what motivated him, stepped into Rachel's room. He waited a moment to let his eyes adjust to the dim light, then walked—okay, *tiptoed,* being mindful of the blinking monitor—to the side of the bassinet. Stood—for how long he didn't know—gazing down at the kid, watching him sleep, and wasn't even aware, just then, that he was holding his breath.

He had to admit the kid had improved with age, although he still didn't think he'd call him *beautiful,* exactly. Then again, seeing him all wrapped up like a papoose in a blue blanket with teddy bears on it, dark hair waving across his scalp, lashes fine as spider webs laying on fat pink cheeks, he could see how a mother might think he was. One tiny hand had managed to break free of the swaddling blanket and was splayed over one cheek, wrinkly fingers spread wide. He reached out with one finger and touched the hand. Instantly, the fingers moved…curled… It reminded him of the way a sea anemone contracted when you poked it with your finger.

The pink mouth contracted, too, drawing up into a tight little bud, and the forehead wrinkled into an infant version of a frown.

J.J. realized, suddenly, that he was smiling.

What the hell am I doing? He jerked his hand back, turned and tiptoed quickly across the room and through the French doors.

Rachel was in the courtyard, standing by the fountain. She was gazing down at the hand she was trailing in the water, but looked up quickly when he stepped onto the veranda, reminding him of a doe startled at a waterhole. She broke into a smile when she saw him, eyes bright and cheeks flushed, and it occurred to him she looked as guilty as he felt.

"Hi," he said. "Back already?"

At almost the same moment, she nodded toward the room he'd just left and said, "Is he—"

He shook his head. His heart was thumping. "Sound asleep."

"Oh." For an instant she looked as if she didn't know whether to be glad or sorry. Then, smiling again, she burst out, "Oh, I had the best—" just as he was saying, "How did your—" So he stopped and motioned for her to continue.

She did, breathless as a child. "Oh, Jethro, you should have seen it, there are just babies *everywhere.* I guess that's the way it is, in the spring, on a farm. Baby calves—there's even a little tiny calf Sage said they have to feed with a bottle because he was a twin and his mother rejected him, but that's only until they get him strong enough, then he said they'll let him nurse one of the milk cows. They are so pretty...the calves are. They seem so shiny and new, and they have such beautiful eyes. There are baby lambs, too, and baby goats—the goats and sheep don't seem to mind twins. Almost all of them have twins, and one of the goats even has triplets. They aren't out in the pasture—they have to stay in pens until the babies are bigger, because of coyotes. Even bears and mountain lions, sometimes, can you imagine? And there's a litter of kittens— Sage said they were born in the haystack, but he moved them into the tack room because they're safer there. They're just getting their eyes open now. I can't wait to see them when they start running around. Oh—and the house is fascinating, too. It's over one hundred years old, made of adobe. The walls must be a foot thick. Sage said—"

"I'm glad you enjoyed yourself," J.J. interrupted, mainly because he didn't think he could stand hearing "Sage said" one more time. "I hate to stop you there—you'll have to tell me all about it some other time. Right now, I'm fixin' to head down the mountain, see if I can pick you up a cell phone."

Her lips twitched and her dimple threatened. "'Fixin' to'—that's Southern, right?"

He grunted. "Funny. Look, I was just wondering if there's anything you need me to pick up for you while I'm down there."

"Oh—yeah." She pressed a hand to her forehead, smoothing back damp wisps of hair. And his stomach clenched as he flashed on an image of his own hand smoothing those same damp wisps while he growled at her, *One more time…come on, baby, you can do it…one more.* "I made a list—Josie has it…"

"Might as well save her the trip." He motioned for her to stay put. "I'll get it from her." He started on across the courtyard, then reversed direction when he remembered he still needed to get his hat. Then halted again and turned back to her, feeling awkward as a tongue-tied kid. "Uh…any particular kind of cell phone? Color? Bells and whistles?"

She shook her head, smiling crookedly and without the dimple. "I don't need fancy. Just need it to work."

He nodded and stepped across the veranda, boots scraping on the stone pavers.

Rachel watched him go, one hand pressed against her pounding heart. She waited until he'd disappeared into his room before letting out the breath she'd been holding.

Thank God I have quieter shoes than he does, she thought. *Otherwise, he'd surely have heard me. If he knew I'd seen him...knew I'd witnessed that moment...him with Sean...he might never forgive me.*

Oh, but I did see it. And I'm so very glad I did.

Chapter 11

She was prepared for him, that night.

She'd brushed her hair, for one thing, and made sure to put on a clean shirt and pants, the cotton knit ones with the elastic waistband Katie had given her to wear while she was getting her figure back. And how long was that supposed to take, she wondered as she surveyed herself in the mirrored closet doors in her room, standing sideways and trying very hard to suck in her stomach. Granted, it hadn't even been a week, yet, but still…

Who am I kidding? And why should I care? With a sigh, Rachel let her cotton knit tunic top fall back into place, covering her billowing breasts and stomach bulges. Not a chance in hell any man was going to find *that* attractive, which was probably for the best, anyway. Sure, Sheriff Jethro Fox was attractive, and given that he'd saved her life and Sean's, too, it was understandable that she might develop some feelings for him. But the timing was all wrong. And, she devoutly hoped, she'd learned a few lessons from past experiences about following where her emotions led too impulsively.

With those emotions firmly in hand, she turned to the bed where Sean lay kicking, squirming, snuffling and gnawing on his fist, not yet worked up to full cry. Murmuring soothing promises, she picked him up and tucked him in the crook of her arm, then opened the door and stepped into the hallway. In the soft glow of the sconces high on the wall she could see J.J.'s door was closed. She hadn't meant to look but couldn't help it as she turned the other way and headed for the kitchen. Just as well, she reminded herself. *Remember?*

In the softly lit kitchen, she marched with confidence to the refrigerator and took out the package of disposable formula bottles. It was much easier to get one out of the package now that it had been opened.

However, opening the bottle, she found, still took two hands. She struggled with it while Sean worked his way from snuffling to fussing to wailing, coming dangerously close to wailing herself, then thought, *Enough of this.* She plunked the unopened bottle in the sink, sniffed, wiped her eyes and marched out of the kitchen and down the hallway. At J.J.'s door she paused, but Sean's insistent wailing made it easy to summon the courage to raise her hand and knock.

"Jethro," she called moistly, "are you awake? I *need* you."

He'd been listening for her. He hadn't been sleeping, and with his French doors open to the courtyard, he'd heard every restless movement she'd made, and most of Sean's, too. When he'd heard her door open and her bare footsteps retreat down the hallway toward the kitchen, he'd almost gotten up and followed her. *Almost.* Until he'd reminded himself of all the good reasons why it was a bad idea being alone with a beautiful woman wearing very few clothes in the wee lonely hours of the night.

Particularly when she was a potential witness, one he was starting to have some decidedly unprofessional feelings about.

So now here she was, knocking on his door. Telling him she needed him. What was he supposed to do about that? Pretend to be asleep and ignore her? *No way in hell.*

He got up, pulled on the same pair of sweatpants he'd worn the night before, raked back his hair with his fingers and opened the door.

She glared up at him, the tears in her eyes shining golden in the light from the hall sconces. "You *said* I shouldn't have to do this alone. I'm sorry to wake you, but I tried, and I *can't.*"

"Shh," he said, only because he was pretty sure his voice would be too growly for real words. Then, because the need to take her in his arms and comfort her was too great to ignore, he took the baby from her and cuddled him instead.

She gave him a fierce, almost accusing look, muttered, "Thanks…" and turned and marched off toward the kitchen, head down, every step, every line of her body proclaiming wounded pride.

Watching her as he followed, J.J. would have smiled, except the knot of emotions in his chest didn't make him feel much like smiling. What they did make him feel was light-headed and a little scared.

In the kitchen, he made himself comfortable in a chair beside the island as he had the previous night, with Sean in the crook of one elbow, and watched Rachel while she got out the formula bottle and warmed it. Evidently though, for Sean the novelty of staring at J.J.'s face had worn off, because after staring at it for a couple of seconds, the kid went back to snorting and squirming and making unhappy faces. So, J.J. gave him the tip of his little finger to suck on.

"What?" he said when he saw Rachel looking at him openmouthed—with alarm, maybe, or horror. "Never hurt my sister's kids any." He looked down at Sean, now sucking greedily on the finger. "Maybe you ought to get him a pacifier."

"I'll put it on the list," she said absently, apparently unable to take her eyes off the awful sight of her child sucking away on his pinky finger. But after a moment she gave herself a little shake and turned back to the sink, picked up the bottle, tested it on her arm then brought it over and handed it to him.

Sean wasn't any too happy about losing the "pacifier" he'd been sucking on, and for a moment or two didn't seem to know what to do with the nipple it was being replaced with. Which prompted J.J. to growl at him in what probably qualified as baby talk. "Yeah…you kinda liked ol' Jethro's finger, didn't you, little guy?"

Rachel gave a liquid-sounding laugh. She pulled out the chair next to him and hitched herself onto it, somewhat gingerly, he noticed.

"Sore?" he asked, without thinking. Then, having bitten down on his tongue in remorse, muttered, "Sorry."

How is this possible? Rachel thought. *Shouldn't there be hormones of some kind that would block feelings like these? It can't be normal, can it, to be so attracted to a man, when my body is still battered and bleeding from giving birth? When at this point, I'm not even sure I could stand to have a man touch me?*

A moot question, she reminded herself, considering in her present shape she couldn't imagine any man *wanting* to touch her.

She cleared her throat. "It's okay. I don't think my body has any secrets from you, anyway."

His gaze was sleepy, heavy-lidded. And for some reason her heart responded by beating faster. "Oh, I don't know about that," he said, in a voice like a tiger's purr. "I think there are all sorts of secrets that body of yours has.…"

Her cheeks burned. Did she imagine it, the unspoken finish: ...*I'd like to explore...?*

She stared back at him, unable to speak or move, the silence in the kitchen broken only by the squeaky sounds Sean made, nursing greedily at the bottle. J.J.'s gray-green eyes seemed almost smoky, and she kept looking into them, desperately afraid if she stopped, her eyes might just travel anywhere they pleased...to his lips, maybe, and then on down to his neck... his throat...his chest. And she would think about...wonder about what it would feel like, touching him.

She leaned her elbow on the island top and propped her cheek in her hand. Feigning a yawn, she murmured, "Jethro, are you ever going to tell me what the other J stands for?"

He dropped his gaze to the baby in his lap, and she saw a smile—a small one—touch his lips. "No big secret," he drawled. After a pause, he came out with it, elongating it into a kind of growl. *"Jefferson."*

"Jefferson. Huh. Well, that's not so bad. You had me thinking it was something awful."

He gave a dry laugh. "Yeah, well, Jethro Jefferson—that's bad enough when you're a little kid."

"Why didn't you go by Jeff?"

"Seems my dad had that one spoken for."

"Ah. So you're a junior?"

"Worse than that. I'm a *third*." He set the formula bottle on the island top, shifted Sean to his shoulder and began to pat his back.

Lord help me, she thought. *I could easily fall in love with this guy.*

"Wow," she said faintly, "Jethro Jefferson Fox, the Third."

"They do things like that in the South." His grin was wry. "So, my mom called me Jethro when I was a kid. Then for a while I got nicknamed Jet—that was when I was playing football in high school. I was a running back, and had some speed in those days, so…I guess it seemed kind of appropriate."

"Jet's kind of cool. So why didn't you keep that nickname?"

He hitched a shoulder, the one not supporting Sean's lolling head. "I don't know, when I got to L.A. it seemed a little bit too…you know, Southern. Too…Tennessee Williams."

Rachel raised her eyebrows at the literary reference, but didn't comment. After a moment, she shook her head and murmured, "James Dean."

"What?"

"Not Tennessee Williams—James Dean. He was Jett Rink in the movie, *Giant*. You know—Texas? Oil millionaire? Rock Hudson…Elizabeth Taylor…"

"That's an old one." His eyes twinkled with teasing lights.

She found herself smiling back at him. "What can I say? I saw it with my grandmother."

"But that wasn't a John Wayne movie."

"We didn't just watch John Wayne movies." The kitchen was warm and quiet and filled with soft golden light and the smells that lingered from dinner the evening before. She felt secure and comfortable in a way she hadn't felt since she was a child, and the anxieties of her adult life seemed far, far away, only a distant murmur like the sounds of surf outside the windows of a well-built house. She stifled a yawn and mumbled, "Anyway, you don't remind me of him anymore, now that I met someone who really does—"

A loud burp interrupted her. J.J. came bolt upright in his chair, one hand going to support Sean's head. He was swearing under his breath.

Rachel lurched to her feet. "Oh, no. Did he—"

"Yeah, he did. Get a towel. Something."

She was already at the sink, running warm water over a dish towel. She squeezed most of the water out and thrust the towel at J.J., who shrugged it off with a jerk of his head as he balanced a now-somnolent and very satisfied-looking infant in both hands.

"It's all down my back. See if you can—"

"Oh, God—I'm so sorry. Let me see—"

"What are you sorry for? *You* didn't upchuck all over me."

She made an ambiguous sound, part laugh and part moan. He shifted in the chair and dipped one shoulder obligingly, and she stepped closer so she could see where the splotch of curdled formula had splattered down his back. His well-muscled, nicely sculpted, lightly tanned back. She reached awkwardly to dab at the spit-up with the wet towel, and her breast bumped against his arm. His well-muscled, nicely sculpted...

She gasped and whispered, "Sorry."

He turned his head and from inches away his eyes burned into hers. "What for?"

"I, um…didn't mean to bump you."

His lips moved. At such close quarters she couldn't be sure, since they were just beyond her field of vision, but she thought they formed a smile. "I don't think you did any permanent damage."

She laughed, a tiny whimper of sound her fingers tried to stifle. Then she needed to speak, and there seemed to be no place to put that hand that wasn't a part of *him*. It fluttered between them like a drunken moth as she fumbled for words. "I'm not used to such—they're so much bigger now…"

"I guess that's pretty normal. What with nursing, and uh… you know."

His voice was a rocky rumble she could *feel*, and she realized her hand, the one holding the towel, was resting, idle, on his back. And that his skin was warm and smooth beneath her fingers, and that she could feel the thumping of his heart.

The heat from his body was like a fur wrap, enveloping her… drawing her closer. But she was already too close…so close, she knew it would take very little—almost nothing—to touch her lips to his.

I want to kiss him. What would happen if I did?

She wondered…and was afraid to take the risk. Until it occurred to her that seconds had ticked by—and seconds were eons long in that time—and he hadn't moved. His eyes still blazed into hers, and his heartbeat…

His heartbeat was a tattoo against her palm, hard and fast, as fast as hers.

Is it possible? Can it be he finds me attractive, even the way I look now, even after all he's seen?

Get real, the voice of reason said inside her head. And another voice answered, *Why not find out? Are you brave enough to take the chance?*

Between the thought and the action there was no time at all. Space, perhaps, for one almost indistinguishable catch in her breathing…and then her lips were touching his, and the shape of his mouth, its texture and warmth, were an anticipated delight—like opening a birthday present and finding within the very thing most desired.

He didn't pull away, and joy surged inside her; her lips curved tremulously into a smile. The unoccupied hand that had wanted so badly to touch him now did so, coming to rest along the side of his face. The roughness of his beard seemed familiar to her, somehow, as if touching him like this was something she'd imagined doing for a long, long time.

Time.

Seconds, she discovered, could last for eons, but they could also be the briefest of moments. For just such a flash of time, she felt his mouth soften…cling to hers…breath whisper from parted lips. Then…she was left trembling, with nothing but space and coldness where the warmth had been.

He cleared his throat, muttered something she couldn't hear. She jerked back, the towel, smelling of baby formula, pressed to her lips.

"Sorry," he said in his gravel-filled voice.

What for? I don't think you did any permanent damage. Did I damage you? She wanted to hurl that at him. Mocking him. Instead, she let him place her baby in her arms. And didn't say a word, not even to ask him something as adult and reasonable as, *What's with the mixed signals, you...jerk?*

"Really," he said, his eyes locking onto hers, narrowed and glittering so that whatever emotions might have been behind them were hidden from her. "I'm sorry—won't happen again." He paused, seemed to collect himself, grunted, "See you in the morning," and left her standing there, rigid, with her cheeks burning and her body cold as ice.

"I'd like to go riding today," Rachel announced at breakfast.

J.J. set his coffee cup down—carefully. Josie, having just refilled his cup, paused with the coffeepot in one hand to give her a look—not of doubt, exactly, but certainly of some concern.

"I feel fine," Rachel said to Josie, well aware she was avoiding looking at J.J. directly. "It's been almost a week, and I didn't have any stitches or tearing." She didn't falter when she saw J.J. wince. Quite clearly. "And I don't plan on running any races or jumping over fences. I seriously doubt Sage would put me on a bucking bronco, so...if you wouldn't mind looking after Sean for an hour or so this morning..."

"Of course, I don't mind. And all of our horses are gentle. And very well trained," Josie said with a smile and a glance at J.J. "Sage trained them himself. He has a 'way' with horses. I'll call him and tell him to saddle one for you."

"Tell him to make that two," J.J. said.

"There's no need for you to go," Rachel said, as Josie's smile brightened. She picked up her cup of Ovaltine and drank, lashes lowered. "If you really don't trust me to go alone, Sage can come with me."

"Oh, but I think—" Josie began.

"J.J. is afraid of horses," Rachel solemnly explained.

J.J.'s coffee cup hit the table with a metallic clang. "Just because I don't like to ride doesn't mean I'm afraid of horses. I can ride a damn horse." He shoved back his chair and stood up. At the door to the kitchen he paused to fire a parting shot over his shoulder. "I'll be ready whenever you are. And don't even think about going without me."

Josie stared after him, started to follow, then came back to the table. Rachel picked up her cup and drank more Ovaltine to hide the fact that she was shaking inside.

"I think you hurt his feelings," Josie said.

Rachel licked her lips and cleared her throat. "I don't think he has feelings," she said carefully.

Josie set the coffeepot on the table. "What makes you say that?"

"If he does, I have no idea what they are. He sure doesn't show any to me."

"Well, of course he doesn't."

Rachel shot Josie a look. "What do you mean by that?"

Josie folded her arms across her waist and fingered a button on the front of her blouse. She closed her eyes for a moment, then said, "Okay, I wasn't going to say anything, especially after you told me—I thought you would...I don't know, figure things out for yourself, but maybe..." She took a breath. "You really don't know?"

"Know what?"

"He's in love with you," Josie said.

Rachel felt as if she'd been struck. Then she had an absurd impulse to laugh. Her mouth was dry, and her pulse was jumping in surprising places. She said faintly, "What makes you say a thing like that? We hardly know each other."

Josie pulled out a chair and perched on the edge of it. "It's obvious. The way he looks at you—" Her mouth tilted wryly in what wasn't quite a smile. "I know what a man in love looks like, and trust me—he is in love with you."

For a moment—just a moment—she let herself believe in the possibility. If—and it was a huge *if*—he could find her attractive, then why not? But how could he? He'd been in love many times, he'd said so himself. What on earth would make him even consider a woman with giant seeping breasts and a flabby stomach?

"How could he be?" she said to Josie, in a hard, flat voice. She swept a hand downward across herself. "Look at me. My body is completely unappealing. And even if I looked like…like something else, clearly—there's not going to be any possibility of sex, not in the immediate future, anyway. What man would bother?"

"Oh, my." Josie closed her eyes briefly, then smiled. "But, isn't that every woman's fantasy, to have a man love her for reasons that don't involve sex? I'll bet that if you were to ask almost any woman what she wants most from a man, it would be that he will love her for who she is, as she is, not for what she looks like, and how available the sex is."

Rachel was silent, thinking of Nicholas, who had almost certainly loved her for her looks and for the sex.

She tried to swallow around the ache in her throat, and it made a sticky sound. "He sure doesn't act like it," she muttered.

Josie waved her hand impatiently. "Of course he doesn't. I'm sure he thinks it's the last thing you would want—or need. You lost your husband not so long ago, and you just had his baby. You're a new mother and a grieving widow." She paused to give Rachel a searching look. "You are, aren't you?"

Rachel swallowed again, but the ache in her throat stayed the same. To her dismay, she heard herself mumble, "I thought I was. Lately I haven't been so sure—"

"Sure of what, dear?"

She took a breath. "Sure that what I had is worth grieving for. I mean, I thought I loved my husband." She glared fiercely at Josie, then covered her eyes with her hand. "I *did*. But lately, especially since—"

"Since…?" Josie prompted again.

"Since I've been around J.J.," Rachel said, her voice barely audible, "and the way he treats me…the way I feel." She looked up, her eyes burning with misery. "Now, I'm wondering if I ever even knew what love is."

Josie made a scoffing sound. "Who does? Some people are lucky, maybe, and get it right the first try. Some of us have to make a few mistakes before we figure it out. But when you do…" Josie's smile was gentle. And enigmatic. "I think you'll know. I know I did."

Rachel stared at her and touched away a tear from her own cheek while her mind swirled with questions. But before she could put one into words, the cell phone in Josie's pocket played a sweet, minor tune.

"That's Sage now," Josie said, reaching for it. "I'll ask him about the horses."

Murmuring into the phone, she rose, picked up the coffeepot and disappeared into the kitchen, leaving Rachel to wonder if this was how it felt to be blindsided by a truck.

"You really don't have to do this, you know," Rachel said.

It wasn't the first time she'd said it, so J.J. didn't bother to reply. He did look over at her though, because he couldn't help it. It wasn't the first time he'd done that, either, and he still thought she looked so damn cute on the back of that horse, a black appaloosa with a spotted white rump and a glossy black mane and tail. She was wearing a pink ball cap Josie had loaned her, and her hair was pulled up in a ponytail that stuck out through the hole in the back of the cap and cascaded down her back in a pretty close match to the horse's tail. She had on jeans and a top made of some flowery silky material that gathered in under her breasts and hung loosely down past her waist and left her arms and a good bit of her chest and back bare. Her skin was flawless, and the color of vanilla ice cream.

"I hope you remembered to put on sunblock," he said.

She smiled at him, showing her dimple. "I did. Did you?"

"Got my hat," he said, giving her a smile back, one a good bit darker than her own. "And my shades. That's all I need."

"You should be careful, you know," she replied, drifting closer to him to give him a critical once-over. "Out in the desert, with your blond hair and fair skin…"

He snorted. "What are you, my mother?" Then he felt like the jerk he was when she just gazed at him with those inscrutable eyes of hers, and he saw just hint of a blush come into her cheeks.

He was glad the aviator shades he was wearing covered his own eyes, because he wasn't sure what she might have been able to read in them. Hunger, maybe? Something for sure that would give away what he was thinking…remembering.

The full, warm weight of your breast pressing against my arm…your hand on my back, fingers moving as if you didn't even know they were…your lips touching mine…your mouth, sweet and soft and deep, there for the taking… If it hadn't been for the baby in my arms, how would I have stopped myself from taking what you offered, even knowing you didn't mean it?

"I'm careful enough," he said gruffly, and added, "Just another reason why I need to get the hell out of the damn desert."

She looked away and didn't answer. They rode along in silence for a while, and J.J. could hear quail calling somewhere off in the hills. Overhead in the cloudless blue, a hawk circled lazily, and closer by, a yellow-and-brown bird flushed out of hiding by Moonshine fluttered up out of the grass and glided away, skimming the tops of the meadow flowers.

He had to admit it wasn't too bad. Not here, not like this. With her.

"It's not so bad, is it?" she asked, as if she'd followed his thoughts.

"What, this? This isn't desert, this is mountains. Sort of."

"No," she said, "I mean the horse. Riding."

He thought about it, flexing his legs in the stirrups to ease the unaccustomed pressure on his backside and eying the view between the horse's two pointy ears down there at the end of its long, long neck. The ears twitched now and then, pointing this way and that, speaking a language all their own, Rachel had told him. He had to admit his horse—a brown one named Misty—had been behaving pretty well, plodding along keeping pace with Rachel's, not showing any inclination to sudden and unexplained leaps or bursts of speed. Hadn't seemed to object to having a strange man on her back. Hadn't tried to throw, kick, trample or bite him, anyway. So far, so good.

"No," he said, "it's not so bad."

He saw her draw a breath and her shoulders relax just a little, and wished he could give her more.

They were riding in an arm of the meadow that extended north beyond the old adobe ranch house and barns, following the creek higher and deeper into the canyon. Where the meadow ended, Sage had told them, a trail continued on into the High Sierras—the part known as the Kern Plateau. There had once been cow camps in those high meadows, accessible only by horseback and pack mule; now there were vacation cabins in some of them, and you could drive there on well-maintained roads. But higher still, only the hiking trails traversed the Sierra Nevada range, past Mt. Whitney, the highest point in the lower forty-eight states, past the groves of Giant Sequoias, all the way to the Cascades and the Oregon border.

Here, as the meadow narrowed down to a ribbon of green, J.J. could smell the sun-warmed pines and feel the cool breezes blowing off of melting snow, and he felt himself growing tense and stubborn, fighting the peace and beauty and grandeur of it. Fighting against the call of the wild, maybe? He didn't know. He only knew he felt angry, and frustrated because he didn't know who or what he was mad it.

I'm a city boy, dammit! I don't care how nice or pretty it is here, it's not where I belong. I belong in the screwed-up, messed-up city, doing what I can to make it a little bit less messed up by rounding up bad people and putting them away. It's what I do, it's who I am. And I want—I need—to get back to it.

"Would you like to stop for a while?"

She was looking at him, a little pleat of concern between her eyebrows. Evidently the shades weren't hiding his thoughts as well as he'd hoped.

"Sure," he said.

Her horse angled off toward the creek without any noticeable instruction from her, and his horse followed along, naturally, without any guidance whatsoever from him. Moonshine, too, appeared ready to take a break from meadow recon, and flopped down in a drift of lupines and stretched out on her side to bask in the sun.

In the shade of the willows along the creek bank, Rachel halted and dismounted with what he thought was amazing grace, given the fact that she was less than a week away from having given birth. She dropped her horse's reins to the ground—Sage had explained the horses were trained to "ground tie," which he gathered meant that as long as the ends of the reins were touching the ground the horse wouldn't run off and leave him stranded. Then she took hold of J.J.'s horse's bridal while he dismounted with something considerably less than grace.

While he was doing stretches and deep-knee bends and trying to work the saddle stiffness out of his legs, Rachel walked both horses down to the creek to let them drink. Then she rubbed them down with a cloth she'd tied onto the back of her saddle, crooning to them in the same tone he'd heard her use with her baby, which gave J.J. an itchy feeling he couldn't find a reason for. He just knew he found it irritating as hell, all that affection and attention being bestowed on a couple of *horses,* for God's sake.

When he thought he could walk without looking like a bow-legged cartoon version of a city slicker, he made his way down to the creek bank, knelt on one knee—trying not to groan audibly—and scooped up some water to wash his face. It was cold as ice. Or melted snow, which it was. When he straightened up, Rachel was standing with one hand on her horse's neck, gazing at him. That same little frown hovered between her eyebrows.

"What?" he said, wiping ice water from his numb face.

She shrugged, but didn't look away. "I was going to ask you the same thing." She took a breath, closed her eyes, then blurted out, "Jethro, what's wrong?"

He could have blustered his way out of it, of course he could have. But something inside him was going still and calm, telling him the moment had come. So he didn't say anything, just looked at her and waited.

She took off her hat, so she wouldn't have to look up at him from under the brim, he supposed. But for him, it just made it harder to look at her; she seemed more vulnerable, somehow, without it.

Holding the hat clutched in one hand, she gave it a little wave and said in a rush, "Is it about last night? The fact that I kissed you? And I know you said sorry, but *I'm* the one that kissed *you*. So I don't know what you had to be sorry about, unless it's because you didn't kiss me back. Is that what you were apologizing for? 'Sorry, but I just don't find you appealing enough to kiss.' Was that it?"

He muttered, "For God's sake, Rachel." But she wasn't through.

"Not that I blame you. I know I'm a fat, flabby mess, and you haven't exactly seen me at my best, and I wouldn't blame you for being completely turned off. So if you don't want to kiss me, or…anything else, I completely—"

He hadn't been aware of moving toward her, but suddenly there he was, close enough to her to take the ball cap from her hand and hook it over the horn of the saddle right behind her. He put his hands on her arms and heard a faint gasp escape her lips.

"You want me to kiss you?" he growled, from deep down in his chest where the emotions lay hidden. "Is that what you want? Because let me tell you, lady, I find you incredibly appealing. More appealing than you can possibly imagine. I can't think of anything I'd like to do more than kiss you— among other things. You understand?"

She just looked at him. He gave her a little shake, and her lips parted. She whispered, "Then why don't you?"

He groaned and looked up into a canopy of pine branches. "Why don't I? Because you have enough crap to deal with, that's why. You're vulnerable and confused. And because you don't know me. You don't know who I am, or what I want from you."

He could hear the faint sound of her swallow. Then her chin

lifted and she looked straight into his eyes. "I know you care about me. You care enough to get on a horse for me. Which I think is *huge*. And maybe I'm not as confused as you think I am. Not anymore. Because I know Nicky would never have done such a thing for me. Never."

For a long moment he stared down at her, hating what had to happen, knowing it had to be now, and that it had to be final. Then he muttered, "Remember, you asked for this." Then he lowered his head and kissed her.

Kissed her. He had in mind something quick and hard, when he started it—something that would send her a message, clear and simple: *Beware of me, little girl, because I'm only going to hurt you.* But then he felt her mouth tremble and soften and open to him, and he knew the only message was the one he was getting, which was that kissing her was what he wanted more than his next breath, and the person most likely to wind up hurt was Jethro Jefferson Fox, the Third.

He hadn't meant to fold her into his arms, which meant raising her up so that her legs just naturally came around him and her arms lifted to twine around his neck. He felt her fingers in the damp hair on the back of his neck, then a rush of coolness as she took off his hat, and somewhere in the back of his mind was an awareness that losing the hat was something like losing a bit of his own armor.

And for that moment, at least, he didn't care. The thinking part of his brain had gone silent, overwhelmed by the part that only *felt*. Felt and wanted *more*. Felt the firm, full press of her breasts against his thumping heart and wanted her skin touching his skin. Tasted the sweet, hot wine of her mouth and longed to taste every inch of her with his mouth. Felt the most tender and womanly part of her body nestled against the hardest and most manly part of his and yearned for the barriers of denim and zippers and buttons that separated them to be *gone*.

It was that yearning that brought him back from the brink. When the swelling of his body became agony, the desire fogging his brain thinned just enough so he could hear the thinking part shrieking at him: *What the hell do you think you're doing? Are you crazy?*

He tried to ignore it for another moment or two, knowing it was going to hurt like bloody hell to tear himself away from her. And it was knowing how he was hurting *her* that made it possible for him, finally, to let her go. He eased her down until her feet were on solid ground again, then took hold of her arms and pulled them away from his neck. Then, he lifted his mouth from hers. Still holding her arms, he gave her a little shake, breathing like a marathon runner. "There—is that what you wanted?"

Her eyes, luminous and wounded, stared up at him. He forced himself to look at her, to see the effects of what he was doing to her—the panting, whimpering breaths, the bruised lips and tear-shimmer—remembering how he'd once wanted to kill the person who'd left bruises on her face, knowing the ones he was leaving were far worse because they were the kind that don't fade.

"You think that's what you want?" He caught several rasping breaths of his own. "Then let me tell you about me. Let me tell you *who I am*."

Chapter 12

"I know who you are," Rachel whispered. Her mind filled with images of his face, his smile as he gazed down at Sean.

He closed his eyes and shook her again, his fingers hard on her arms. She was sure there would be bruises. "You don't," he said harshly. "You only think you do."

"Then I...don't understand."

"I'm a cop—you got that? A *cop*. And you, lady, are the widow of a crime kingpin's son, who happened to be present when your husband was shot along with a couple of federal agents. You were *there*. You're a *witness*. Get it?"

"But I don't—"

He shook her again, and she stopped and just stared at him, wishing she could block out these images: the cold glitter of his eyes, the hard, unyielding line of his mouth. *A moment ago I was kissing that mouth. How could it have felt so good?*

"You're a witness. You're *my* witness. You are the witness who is going to break this case for me. The witness who's going to get me my old job back. Now—do you understand what I want from you?"

She nodded. Her body had gone cold and still. He must have felt it, because he let go of her arms, exhaled and muttered, "Good..." He bent down to pick up his hat from the mossy creek bank where she'd tossed it.

She cleared her throat. "You want me to testify," she said carefully, feeling nothing at all, except cold. "You want me to say I saw who killed those two feds."

He turned to her, having jammed his hat back on his head, and she saw his eyes glint from the deep shadow of the hat's brim. "I want you to tell what you *saw*. What you remember."

Rachel drew a deep breath and pulled together the remnants of her strength, self-respect and pride. "Then I'm going to have to disappoint you," she said, in a voice that didn't shake. "I'm sorry you've had to go through all this for nothing, but I didn't see *anything*. Nicky shoved me down behind a Dumpster. I don't know who killed the law officers. Do you get it? I don't even know who killed Nick." She sucked in another breath. "So, you can go home now."

She plucked the pink cap Josie had given her from the saddle horn, lifted her foot into the stirrup and, ignoring twinges in tender parts of her body, lifted herself into the saddle. From that height she looked down at the man she'd once thought looked like a hero from an old Western movie. He no longer made her think of John Wayne, or anybody else; now, he was just J.J. And, looking down at him, she still didn't feel anything. But she knew the pain was out there, gathering like a tsunami wave, heading straight for her. And she knew that when it hit her she wanted to be far away from the man who had caused it.

"Do you understand?"

He lifted his head and looked at her, his face stony.

"I can't help you. I don't have anything for you, so you don't have any reason to stay."

"Carlos—"

"Sage will protect me. He can hire someone. This is my grandfather's place, and I want you gone."

She tugged on the appaloosa's reins and turned her head toward home. She dug her heels into the mare's sides and leaned forward over her neck. She saw J.J. leap back out of the way as the mare's hooves bit into the moist earth, and then she was surging up the shaded slope and into the meadow. Once on the open ground, she gave the horse her head and took what comfort she could from what should have been one of her greatest pleasures—riding a horse at a flat-out gallop through an open field, with the wind in her face and the sun on her back.

J.J. watched the horse and rider hit the meadow and go thundering toward the barn, two almost identical ponytails streaming like flags in the wind, and felt like throwing his hat to the ground in frustration. How, he wondered, had he managed to botch things so badly? He couldn't have imagined a worse outcome.

A moment later, he wished he could have, because a worse outcome is what he got. His sweet little brown mare lifted up her head, uttered a heart-stopping whinny and took off after her friend, the appaloosa.

So much for ground-tying, J.J. thought. And then, as Moonshine lurched to her feet and went loping up the slope in pursuit of the horses. *Et tu, Moon? What is this—you girls stick together?*

He took off his hat, whacked it against his pants leg a time or two, then put it back on and began to make his way through the pines, swearing bitterly at himself. When he got to the meadow, Moonshine came trotting through the grass to meet him. The dog sat down on her haunches and gave him a long, doleful stare, panting hard, tongue lolling.

"Don't start with me," J.J. warned.

As he watched the two horses and one rider rapidly vanish into the distance at a pace faster than he ever wanted to go on the back of a living creature, he considered he was probably better off walking home.

"Man, I'm sorry," Sage said.

He was in the barn, brushing down the brown horse, Misty, when J.J. got there. Out in the pasture he could see the appaloosa, already placidly grazing. Misty turned her head to look at him with big brown innocent eyes as if to say, "Hey, buddy, what happened to you?" But J.J. wasn't fooled.

He leaned against a stall and folded his arms across his chest. "Yeah, I'm sorry, too."

Sage threw him a look. "It's her place, you're her guest. If she wants you to go…" He shrugged and went back to brushing.

J.J. coughed, straightened up. "You know, it's gonna have to be up to you, now, to keep her safe." Sage nodded. "I mean, I'll do my best to get back here as quick as I can, but…" His plan was to get some backup, some legal authority to hold Rachel, or at least keep her in his protective custody until they could find out what she knew about the shooting. Or until they got enough on Carlos to put him away without her help. Meanwhile… "You got any guns?"

"Couple deer rifles," Sage said. "A shotgun."

"These guys will have automatic weapons," J.J. said.

The house was silent. Entering through the front door, J.J. could see across the courtyard to the veranda, where Rachel sat in the rocker nursing Sean. Since he was pretty sure there was nothing to be gained by another encounter with her, he went through the living room and dining room and into the kitchen, where he found Josie at the sink, stemming a bowlful of strawberries. She glanced up, and he thought he caught the shine of tears in her eyes.

"Sheriff J.J., I'm so sorry," she began.

"Yeah, me, too," he said, cutting her off. "I'll be out of your way, soon as I can. Listen—is there any place in this house you could hide, if you had to?" Josie turned to look fully at him, the back of one hand, the one holding a paring knife, pressed to her nose. "You know—like a basement, or a safe room…"

She hesitated, then nodded and pointed the knife at the ceiling. "In the chapel—down at the other end of the house. There's a secret door. It goes up to the bell tower. It's Sam's—it was Mr. Malone's private place. The only way to get to it is stairs." She twirled the knife to create a picture of a circular staircase.

"That'll do," J.J. said. "Listen—I want you to promise me, okay? If you see any sign of Carlos or his goons, I want you to get Rachel and the baby to that room. Get them up there, barricade the door and call 911. Don't go out or open it for anyone until help arrives. Got it?"

Josie nodded and whispered, "Got it."

He left her standing there looking after him and went down the corridor to his room. He took his duffel bag out of the closet and threw his clothes into it, dumped his traveling toiletry case on top of the clothes and zipped the bag shut. Then he got his service Glock and holster out of the drawer in the nightstand and laid it on the bed. He took out the magazine, checked it, put it back. Did the same with his backup Glock, then put it back in its holster where he always wore it, strapped to his right ankle.

He walked slowly to the French doors and looked out. Rachel was still there, rocking her baby. The way she was sitting he couldn't see her face, and she wouldn't know he was there unless he opened the doors or called to her. Which there wasn't much point in doing. She'd made her feelings plain enough.

For the best, he told himself, ignoring the dull ache in his chest. *Just as well. Last thing you needed...*

He went back to the bed, picked up his duffel bag in one hand and his service pistol in the other and left the house by the same route as he'd entered. Josie, he noticed, was nowhere to be seen.

Outside in the shaded parking area in front of the six-car garage, he opened the door of his pickup and called to Moonshine. When he told her to get in the truck, she looked at him like he'd lost his mind, so he boosted her up by her hind end, tossed the duffel bag in after her and shut the back door. He got into the front, placed the Glock and its holster on the passenger seat, started up the engine and rolled away down the drive.

At the T intersection, he kept going straight, and when he pulled up to the big barn, Sage came strolling out to meet him, the border collie at his heels. J.J. waited for him to come close, then rolled down his window and handed him the Glock.

"You ever fire one of these?" he asked.

"I have not," Sage said.

J.J. showed him how to chamber a round and set the safety. "Keep it on you," he said, looking the other man square in the eyes. "Don't put it in a drawer or hang it on a nail. Put the holster on and wear it."

"Will do," Sage said.

"Goes in the small of your back," J.J. said.

"Got it."

J.J. nodded. "I'll be back as soon as I can. Meanwhile... keep her safe."

Sage nodded. J.J. rolled the window up and drove around in a circle and headed back down the dirt lane.

He was about halfway down the mountain when he saw the chopper go by overhead. He stomped on the brake, rolled down the window and stuck his head out, watching the chopper make its way up the canyon toward the hacienda.

Black chopper, no markings. He could think of only one person it could be.

Carlos Delacorte.

Or his goons, which amounted to the same thing.

He swore, hit the steering wheel with the heel of his hand. Started up the truck. What the hell was he going to do? Couldn't turn around—boulders the size of SUVs on both sides of the road. He had no choice but to keep going until he found a place where he could turn around, and in the meantime...

I'll be too late. Sage with a couple of deer rifles and a Glock against God only knows how many trained killers armed with automatic weapons...

I've as good as killed him. And probably Josie and Rachel, too.

Careening down the rutted dirt road, steering one-handed, he managed to punch in 911 on his cell phone.

"What is the nature of your emergency?"

"This is San Bernardino County Sheriff's Deputy J. J. Fox, requesting immediate assistance."

"I'm sorry, did you say—"

"Listen carefully, and don't interrupt," J.J. yelled into the phone. "I have a code—oh, hell, let me make this easy for you. I have a possible kidnapping in progress, June Canyon Ranch, off Highway 178. Multiple suspects, all armed and dangerous. Need immediate assistance. This is an emergency. If you have a S.W.A.T. team and a chopper, suggest you get 'em in the air—*now*."

"Sir, if you'll just stay on the line—"

"Can't do that. Just get me some help. That's June Canyon Ranch—don't have an address, but it belongs to Sierra Sam Malone. Gotta go." He dropped the cell phone into the center console and took hold of the wheel with both hands. Sent up a prayer and yanked it to the right, steering into a relatively clear patch of sand. Backed up into the resulting dust cloud, shifted into forward gear and hit the gas. Moonshine whined as the truck went bouncing and jouncing up the winding road, back the way they'd come.

Rachel saw the helicopter pass overhead as she sat on the veranda rocking Sean. She knew instantly whose it was. She knew, because she had flown in it—or one just like it—not so long ago. The one that had whisked Nicky and her from their wedding reception at Carlos's Malibu beach house to the airport, where Carlos's private jet had been standing by to fly them off to Tahiti for their honeymoon.

Cold enveloped her. She held on to Sean as if someone might try to rip him from her arms. She didn't remember leaping to her feet or going inside or crossing her room, but when she opened the door, Josie was standing there with her fist raised to knock.

"Carlos—" Rachel gasped.

Josie grabbed her arm, motioning with her other hand. "I thought so. Bring him. Come with me. Hurry."

Rachel followed her blindly, back onto the veranda, then across the sunlit courtyard. The wing of the house opposite the kitchen and living room was higher than the rest of the hacienda. Josie opened arched double doors in the whitewashed wall and motioned Rachel to go in ahead of her. Inside it was cool and dim, and as her eyes adjusted to the light, Rachel saw that they were in a small chapel. Josie gave her no time to get her bearings, but took her arm and urged her to the left, toward a beautifully carved wooded altar. She hurried ahead of her up the steps, reached up and turned a candle sconce on the wall to the right of the altar. To Rachel's bemusement, the altar creaked slowly outward to reveal an opening behind.

"Come," Josie whispered, gesturing urgently. "You'll be safe in here."

Rachel gave a sobbing laugh. Once again, it seemed, she would be putting her trust in Carlos's respect for his Roman Catholic upbringing.

Holding Sean for dear life, she ducked through the opening and found herself at the foot of a wrought-iron staircase that wound upward into shadows. Josie waited for her to begin the climb, then pulled the altar and secret door back into position and secured it with a heavy old-fashioned wooden bar before following.

The stairway ended at a landing, with a single door, also of heavy, old-fashioned wood. Josie opened the door and once again waved Rachel into the room ahead of her before closing and barricading this door, too, with a sturdy wooden bar.

"This is Sam's room," Josie said, breathless with excitement, or from the climb. "It used to be the bell tower, but Sam had the bell taken down. It's mounted on the front patio downstairs."

Rachel nodded, barely listening. There were small windows on three sides of the tiny room, set in walls nearly a foot thick. Other than that, she noticed very little, except that the room was sparsely furnished, with a twin bed covered by an old-fashioned handmade quilt, a nightstand and a straight-backed chair and a small writing desk. There were framed photographs on the walls, but she didn't take the time to look at them. Still holding Sean, she went to join Josie at one of the windows.

The window looked out toward the front of the house. To the left was the curving flagstone walk and shallow steps that led to the front door. Straight ahead, the driveway wound through the stands of poplars and pines before reaching the barbed wire fence that bordered the meadow pasture and arrowing off to the right toward the old ranch house and barns. From this vantage point, they had a clear view of the meadow, and the black helicopter that was just settling onto it like a dragonfly onto a pond.

Sage was in the house, standing in front of the open gun safe, when he heard the chopper fly over. He went to the window and watched the black bird hover, then set itself down in the meadow across from the big house. He was pretty sure the chopper didn't belong to anybody he wanted to see.

He went back to the safe and took out the only weapon that was inside. Then he got out a box of shotgun shells, loaded the gun and put a handful of cartridges in his shirt pocket. The rifles were gone, both of them, and he knew who had them. No use wishing for what wasn't there. He knew the shotgun wasn't going to be much good against assault rifles, but he figured it might come in handy at close range, if it came to that.

He went to the front door and whistled for the dog. He came bounding from the direction of the barn, evidently excited over the prospect of visitors from the sky. Sage held the door open for him, said, "Stay, dog," and shut him inside.

He could hear the dog whimpering as he set out for the big house at a dead run, cradling the shotgun in one arm while he pulled the Glock out of its holster in the small of his back with the other.

He was outnumbered and outgunned, but he had knowledge of the terrain on his side. That, and maybe the instincts of his ancestors. If he could make it to the trees, he figured he could flit from tree to tree, picking the gunmen off one by one as they came up the lane. He'd seen a documentary one time about how the Natives had shown the American colonists how to fight like that against the British. It had evidently worked for them, so he figured he had as good a shot as any at holding off these guys until help arrived.

Only one problem. There was a stretch of open ground along the road to get across before he reached the cover of the trees.

Even so, he almost made it. He was about fifty yards from safety when he heard the first shots. He didn't fire back, figuring it would just waste what ammo he had, just put his head down and ran like the wind, praying all the way. The bullet hit him just as he reached the trees. It didn't hurt, just felt like someone had whacked him with a shovel. He spun around and the shotgun went flying, but he held onto the Glock as he crashed onto the pine-needle cushioned ground.

High in the bell tower, Josie uttered a sound like a wounded animal and clamped her hand over her mouth.

Rachel felt as though she'd been slugged in the stomach. Breath gusted from her lungs; instinctively, she tightened her arms around Sean. *Oh God, oh God, oh God,* was all she could think, at first. Then: *I can't let this happen!*

Turning, she thrust her baby at Josie. "Here—please. Keep him safe—"

Cradling Sean in one arm, Josie caught at her shirt. "Wait—no—you can't." Tears were streaming down her face. "You have to stay here. J.J. said—"

Breathless, Rachel shook her head. "No—no, it's okay. It's Sean they want. If I go out there without him, they won't kill me. Not until they make me tell them where he is." She gave the other woman a quick hug and slipped from her grasp. At the door, she lifted the bar, opened it and ran down the stairs, footsteps echoing loudly on the metal steps. At the barricaded door to the chapel she paused to gasp for breath, one hand going to the cheek that no longer bore any trace of the bruises Carlos's fist had put there. She felt cold…like throwing up. He would beat her, she was sure. He'd hit her for a letter she'd hidden from him; what would he do to her for hiding his grandson?

She saw again, in super slow-motion, Sage whirling around from the impact of the bullet, then crashing to the ground. Tears blurred her vision.

I'm sorry, Jethro. This is my fault. I should never have sent you away.

She dashed away the tears, took a deep breath and lifted the heavy bar and pushed the altar back far enough so she could slip through the opening. She shoved the altar back into place, ran through the chapel and out the arched double doors, across the courtyard to the front entry. On the front steps, she hesitated. Through the trees, out in the meadow she could see three men dressed in black making their way slowly toward the fence. They all held automatic weapons, ready to fire.

She pressed her hand against her wildly thumping heart, gasped in a breath, and ran down the lane, waving her arms and screaming, "Wait—don't shoot! Don't shoot!"

She didn't wait to see what the gunmen's response to her cry might be, but ran on between the towering trees. Just before the trees ended and the lane straightened to run parallel to the fence, she saw Sage. Relief overwhelmed her when she saw that he was sitting upright, his back against a tree trunk. He held a gun in his hand. When he saw her, he struggled to rise, and called out to her in a voice like the croaking sound a crow makes.

"Rachel! Rachel—no!"

She ignored him and ran on. At the fence—that damned barbed wire fence—she halted, holding on to the top wire, and yelled across to the advancing gunmen. "Let me talk to Carlos. If he's with you, let me talk to him!"

The gunmen slowed, then stopped, weapons pointing straight at her. Her heart was racing so fast, she wasn't sure she could make a sound, but somehow she heard herself yell, "Tell Carlos, I've hidden the baby where he'll never find him. If he wants to see his grandson, he'll have to talk to me."

One of the gunmen put his hand to his ear, then nodded at his comrades. He started toward her while the other two stayed where they were. Shaking with hope and fear, Rachel bent over and began the tricky process of climbing through the fence.

From somewhere on the edges of her consciousness she heard a powerful engine revving…the screech of tires. Someone shouted, called out her name, but she didn't pause. Out in the meadow, the two gunmen raised their guns.

Then all hell broke loose. And Rachel was caught in the middle of it—literally. Hung up in a barbed wire fence.

Barreling along the lane, J.J. could barely see through the dust cloud he was raising. But he saw Rachel. Saw her come flying out of the shelter of the trees into the open, waving her arms. At first he thought she'd lost her mind. Then, that she was waving at him. Then he saw she was heading straight for three thugs armed with assault rifles. *What the hell?*

When he saw her bend down and start to climb through the fence, and one of the gunmen lower his rifle and start toward her, his heart nearly stopped. Part of him was so furious with her he could have killed her himself. The other part…the biggest part was so terrified he felt paralyzed.

As he brought the pickup to a jolting halt, he caught movement from just beyond the horrifying scene being played out by the fence. He opened the door and dove out, telling Moon to stay put as he slammed the door shut. Crouched by the front fender, he could see Sage ahead in the trees, pulling himself upright with his back against the trunk of a tall pine. His shirt was stained dark and his right arm hung limp at his side. In his left hand was J.J.'s Glock. He waved the Glock at J.J. and made a jerking motion toward the meadow with his head.

J.J. got the message. *Go get her. I'll cover you.*

He nodded. Ran in a crouch around the front of his truck and headed for Rachel, who was still bent over in the middle of the barbed wire fence. He got to her about the same time Delacorte's goon did.

The goon halted and leveled his gun at J.J., who was wishing he'd unholstered his backup Glock before dashing to Rachel's rescue. It was the kind of rookie mistake that could cost a man his life. And was about to cost him his.

In the next fraction of a second, he saw the goon's gun go flying out of his hands. The man screamed and grabbed his thigh, and went down with blood squirting from a bullet hole in his pants leg.

Thanks, Sage. I always knew you'd be a good man to have on my side in a fight.

Out in the meadow, the other two gunmen had opened fire. J.J. grabbed Rachel and hauled her out of the fence, ignoring the sounds of ripping cloth. He had her almost back to the cover of his truck when he felt his right leg go out from under him. He caught hold of the front bumper to keep from going down, all but threw Rachel behind the front tire, then dove headfirst after her. He couldn't feel his right foot, but was afraid to look at it, pretty sure he wasn't going to like what he saw.

"You're hurt," Rachel confirmed. She was on her knees beside him, her cheeks streaked with tears and dust. Her eyes, he saw, were glassy with shock.

J.J. grunted. He was too busy trying to get his backup Glock out of the holster on his wounded leg to reply.

* * *

Sam Malone was making his way along the creek, heading toward the old ranch house, when he saw the black chopper beating its way up the canyon. He watched it hover over the meadow, then drop out of sight behind the barn.

"Don't much like the look of that, Ol' Paint," he said to the horse, who twitched his ears in reply. Sam urged the painted horse into a gallop.

Keeping the barns between himself and whatever was going on out in his meadow, he didn't see the gunmen get out of the chopper and head for his house. He didn't see Sage go dashing up the lane. But he heard the sound of gunfire. That was when he pulled up in the shelter of the corrals and unbuckled the leather flap that held his hunting rifle in its saddle holster. The rifle was a favorite of his, a nice old Winchester bolt-action—not fancy, but it would do the job. He loaded a magazine, threw the bolt a couple of times, then laid the rifle across his lap and said, "Let's go, Paint."

He came out of the shelter of the barn unnoticed, and saw Rachel come running down the driveway, yelling and waving her arms. He saw her stoop down to climb through the fence. He saw the sheriff's pickup truck go barreling along the lane, screech to a halt, and the sheriff jump out and run to Rachel. He let out a cackle of approval.

Then he saw the guy closest to the fence go down, and the two out in the meadow raise their guns. He saw J.J. grab Rachel and run for his truck in a hail of gunfire. And he saw him go down. He didn't see Sage, not then. But rage filled him.

I'm not letting those hoodlums hurt our granddaughter, Elizabeth!

A breeze skirled through the corral, raising dust. It brought a whisper. *What do you think you can do to stop it, old man?*

"I may be old, but I can still ride, and I can still shoot!"

He looped the reins around the saddle horn, shouldered the Winchester, dug his heels into the painted horse's sides and said, "Come on, *Paint!*"

Once clear of the corral fences, Sam Malone gave a blood-curdling yell, and horse and rider went hurtling across the meadow toward the advancing gunmen, Sam firing the rifle as he rode.

The two gunmen never saw them coming.

It was Rachel's nightmare playing out in broad daylight.

Gunfire, the smell of blood and gasoline...but I'm lying in dust and trampled grass, not wet and grimy pavement. No gleaming asphalt and flashing lights. The sun is hot on my scalp. I see Nicky's bloody hand as he pulls up his pants leg and unbuckles—no, not Nicky. It's J.J. who unbuckles the gun from his ankle, which is bloody and turned the wrong way.

Or is it?

Everything was chaos, happening either in slow motion or too fast to take in.

Crouched down beside J.J. with her hands over her ears in a vain attempt to drown out the gunshots, Rachel heard a terrible sound. A blood-curdling yell that stirred the hair on the back of her neck. She'd heard that sound before. She'd heard it in those old western movies she'd watched with her grandmother.

Impossible. And yet.

It was an Indian war cry, straight out of Old Hollywood, if not actual history.

Flat on her belly, she peered under the truck and knew she must be dreaming. She'd been shot, perhaps, and hadn't realized it. Now she was delirious, or dying.

Out in the meadow, suspended in heat shimmer, a rider on a painted horse was bearing down on the helicopter and the two remaining gunmen. He rode tall in the saddle, hat gone, white hair and beard blowing in the wind, and as he rode, he was firing a rifle and yelling that hair-raising war cry.

J.J. couldn't believe what he was hearing. He had to look. Dragging himself around the front end of the truck, he managed to get himself into position to see what was happening out there in the meadow. And now that he could see it, he still couldn't believe it.

From out of nowhere, it seemed, came a horse and rider at full gallop, straight into the face of the two men armed with assault rifles. The man had white hair and a beard, and was riding no-handed, firing a bolt-action rifle and yelling like a banshee. A one-man cavalry charge.

The two gunmen seemed to freeze—in a state of shock, probably. Then they both ran for the chopper. They had barely scrambled aboard before the chopper lifted off. The old man on the horse waited calmly, rifle raised, as the chopper launched into the air. He took careful aim, following the chopper's flight, and fired. Threw the bolt and fired again. The chopper seemed to hesitate. Then it wobbled, dipped to one side, plunged straight down into the meadow grass and erupted in a ball of flame.

J.J. had ducked instinctively and covered his head when the chopper crashed. When he raised it and looked out on the meadow, at first he couldn't see anything through the billowing black smoke. Then the smoke finally lifted, and it was clear that both the horse and rider had vanished.

For a moment he just leaned his head back against the bumper, fighting nausea and darkness. He was losing a lot of blood, he knew that. And he had no idea how bad off Sage was. But first, there was Rachel.

She was crying, sobbing, tears pouring down her face like

rain. He crawled over to her and when he gathered her into his arms, she kept sobbing, "It was Nicky…it was Nicky…"

"Shh…not Nicky, sweetheart—Carlos," he croaked. "It was Carlos. But he's dead. They're all dead. You're safe now. You're safe…"

That was all he remembered.

Everything was the same. It had been exactly four weeks since she'd been there—three since what the newspapers had been calling The Shootout at June Canyon Ranch. Once again, a three-quarter moon hung high in the cloudless sky, extinguishing the stars and casting shadows across the land. And the hound dog named Moonshine kept her vigil on the barren rise in front of the trailer.

Rachel stopped her car—she'd bought a new one, a hybrid, to replace the BMW Nicky had given her—and once again, hesitated before getting out. Not because she was afraid of the dog, who had risen, tail wagging, to greet her. This time, it was the man in front of the trailer she was wary of. She could see him sitting in the folding chair under the string of Christmas lights, his guitar across his lap, watching her. When she saw him set the guitar aside, she opened the door and got out of the car.

Moonshine whined and shifted her feet eagerly. Rachel bent down to hug her and got a lick across her face in welcome. Ah yes, she remembered that tongue. That smell.

Wiping her face with the sleeve of the jacket she'd put on—it could get chilly in the desert, at night, even this late in the spring—she walked toward the trailer, self-conscious under J.J.'s unwavering gaze. He didn't get up, and when she got closer she saw that he had his bandaged leg propped on an overturned bucket. A pair of crutches leaned against the wooden stairs within easy reach.

"Hello," he said, nodding.

"You don't seem surprised to see me," Rachel said, leaning against the stairs next to the crutches because her legs didn't feel steady. "I suppose Katie called you."

He shifted, rocking back so he could look up at her, hands relaxed on the arms of the chair. "Nah," he said, "I've been kind of wondering what was taking you so long."

There was silence, then, while they looked at each other. Her heart hammered and her mouth had gone dry. She thought he still looked like a Western movie hero—hair still shaggy, beard once again grown beyond fashionable shadow. But there was something different about him…something about his eyes, she decided. He'd lost the cop-look. Tonight, he was just a man.

My man.

"You could have come back to the ranch," she said in a thickened voice. She was determined not to cry.

"Wanted to give you time." His voice sounded odd, and she wondered if he, too, was holding back emotions he wasn't ready to show.

She straightened restlessly. "Time? For what?"

He shrugged. "To heal. Think."

I don't need to think. I know what I want, Jethro.

She took a breath. "Speaking of healing, how's your leg coming along?

"It's…coming along."

"I heard you've had two surgeries on it already."

He nodded. "Yeah, they've got it full of a bunch of rods and pins. I guess next month they'll be grafting in some bone from somewhere else to replace what the bullet took out."

"So…how long before…?"

"Before I'm back on two feet? At least ten months, they tell me. But hey—at least I've still got two. There was some doubt about that, for a while." She could see the white shine of his grin.

Her own smile struggled, and died half-born.

"How's Sage doing?" J.J. asked.

"Good." She sat down on the next to bottom step and leaned her cheek on one hand. "His was a flesh wound— bullet went right through his shoulder. No broken bones. He'll have a couple of gnarly scars, but otherwise he's pretty much healed."

"Glad to hear it." There was a long pause, and then in a hardened voice, "You know Carlos is dead."

She sucked in a breath and let it out. "I know. I heard." The DNA report on the bodies recovered from the wreckage of the helicopter had finally come in. The bodies had officially been identified as those of Carlos Delacorte, two of his bodyguards, and the pilot.

"The third gunman survived," J.J. said. "I hear he's been singing like a bird to the U.S. Attorney. They tell me Delacorte's organization is folding like a house of cards."

Rachel nodded. The silence came again.

J.J. cleared his throat. "How's Sean?"

She straightened up with a smile. "He's great. Growing like a weed, as they say." She paused. "He's at Katie's. She's keeping him for the night."

"For the night?"

She turned her head to look at him. "That's what I said." And she managed to hold the look through another long silence.

His voice came softly. "Rachel, are you sure you know what you're doing?"

She shifted impatiently. "I'm a fairly intelligent woman, Jethro. I like to think that when I make a mistake, I learn from it. So I don't make the same one again. I made a doozy of one with Nicholas, and as a result I think I've learned how to tell a good man from a bad one." She covered her face with her hands, then shook her head as if to clear it. "Nicky was a bad man—I know that, now. He lied to me, J.J. I tried to tell you—that day. When it all happened." She jerked in a breath. "It was Nicky. That's one of the reasons I came. To tell you that…you have your witness. I remembered. It was when I saw you take your gun off of your ankle, I remembered Nicky did the same thing that night. He shoved me down behind the Dumpster, then he took a gun out of his ankle holster and started shooting. He killed them, J.J. My husband killed those two agents. I saw him do it. So…you can close your case. I hope—"

She broke off and looked away, swallowing tears. *I hope it gets you your job back. I hope you get what you want, Jethro. I really do.*

"Thank you," he said softly.

Rachel stood up and brushed at the seat of her pants. His voice came again, buried in gravel now.

"Was that the only reason you came?" He paused, and when she didn't answer, prompted, "You said Katie's got Sean for the night."

"Yes, I did." She closed her eyes, then abruptly turned back to him. "I wanted to ask you a question."

"Shoot. Oops—sorry, bad choice of words." His teeth flashed white again. "Go ahead—ask."

She blurted it out all in a rush, which was the only way she could. "Was that the only reason you stayed with me…took care of me…looked after me? Josie said you were in love with me. I sort of started to believe her. Then…you told me I was just a witness to the murders, and—"

"I never said *just*."

Her heart skipped, then seemed to stop. Holding her breath, she said, "Then I have to know. Now that Carlos's empire is collapsing…now that you have your witness…is there any other reason for me to stay?"

He looked at her for a long time, his face somber in the

festive glow of the Christmas lights. Her heartbeats counted off the seconds. Then, "You're gonna make me say it, aren't you?"

She hitched a shoulder. "Say it, or show me."

"Can't very well show you if you're way over there."

She drew a shaking breath and felt a smile a-borning. "I don't think that chair will hold both of us."

"Then hand me those crutches, dammit. I think I've waited for you long enough."

With a sobbing laugh, she thrust the crutches at him. Then he was upright, and she was pushing past impediments—bucket, crutches, chair—to get to him. With his back braced against the stair railing, he pulled her into his arms.

Words came, stumbling over each other, tangled in hot breaths and frantic kisses.

"I did, didn't I? Wait…long enough—"

"Yes—yes—I just got the doctor's blessing this morning. That's why I didn't come sooner. I wanted—"

"You could have come sooner. I'd have waited. It's not just sex I want from you."

"That's what Josie said—she thought it was romantic. I couldn't believe—"

"Believe it…"

She felt his mouth quiver. He pulled back and touched his own face. "I haven't shaved—"

Small evidences of vulnerability that made her heart ache and grow too big for her chest. Tears she'd been trying so hard not to shed welled up and ran down her cheeks as she reached up to lay her hand on his. "Don't," she whispered brokenly, "you're fine the way you are. I'm not exactly at my best, either, you know. I'm still fat, my stomach's flabby, I have stretch marks and my breasts leak…"

"You're kidding, right?" He held her face between his two hands and gazed down at her as if he were King Midas and she was made of pure gold. "You are the most beautiful woman I've ever seen in my life."

He kissed her then, the way he'd always wanted to, cherishing her with his mouth, telling her that way how he felt because he couldn't seem to do it with words. And then somehow the words came anyway, more easily than he could have imagined. "I love you, Rachel. God, how I do love you."

She laughed, giddy with a kind of happiness she'd thought she'd never know. "And I love you. And…can we go inside now?"

Getting up the stairs and into the trailer was goofy and clumsy and exhilarating and frustrating, and by the time they were safely inside the trailer's tiny bedroom, they were both out of breath and half-mad with desire. They stood beside the bed, kissing and touching each other, laughing, tugging ineptly at buttons and clothing like giddy teenagers.

J.J.'s shirt went first. He shucked it off and let it drop to the floor, then put his hands on Rachel's shoulders. His body shuddered and he exhaled softly as she leaned into him, and he felt her wet cheek lay sweetly on his chest. Stroking her back, feeling her full breasts pillowed against him, he closed his eyes and for just one moment felt a wave of pure terror.

She's so vulnerable…I can't hurt her. How can I do this? What if I screw it up?

"Rachel…honey," he whispered brokenly, "do you want me to turn off the light?"

He felt her sigh. Then she lifted her head and looked up at him, lips already swollen, eyes shining bright and shook her head. "This is me," she said, with a shrug so simple and sweet it made his heart ache. "I think you'd better see what you're getting."

Silently laughing, filled with pain and emotions too overwhelming to bear, he kissed each eyelid…then her mouth.

Then he lifted his head, and made it a point to look only into her eyes while he undressed her, trying to tell her without words that he knew exactly what he was getting, and that the way he felt about her had very little to do with her body or her face, as lovely as they were. When she was naked, he folded her into his arms, all but overcome by the feel of her body against him, and whispered, "I wish..."

But he couldn't finish it. He would have to get better at this business of sharing his innermost thoughts, hopes and desires, he supposed. He planned on spending the rest of his life learning how.

She helped him take off his pants and one shoe and sock, and they laid each other down on the bed, the giddiness and laughter done with now, touching with gentleness and care, exploring each other's body's with tenderness and wonder. Time ceased to have any meaning for him; his only reality was her mouth, her hands, the soft, sweet mystery of her body. They body he'd seen in such different circumstances, and yet, had no knowledge of at all. He felt he could go on like this forever, if that was what she wanted, just touching... exploring...letting her do the same.

Then...he knew he couldn't. Not now.

As if she felt his urgency, without his having to ask her, she slid over him and astride his body with a kind of innate grace he realized he'd seen before. And he found it was intensely erotic, remembering the way she'd mounted the black appaloosa and ridden like the wind....

Looking down into his eyes, Rachel saw them darken with heat and passion, and felt a surge of power and confidence such as she'd never felt in her life before. She eased herself onto him and felt him thrust deep, deep inside her, and wanted to throw back her head and shout with purest joy. Instead, she drew a shaken breath, looked down at the man she'd somehow come to love more than life, twined her fingers with his and whispered his name.

"Jethro…"

In the humid darkness, Rachel stirred against his side.

"Will you come back with me?" she murmured.

He kissed her damp hair. "To the ranch, you mean?"

He felt her nod. "Since you're on leave anyway…"

He laughed softly. "Oh, yes, I'd like to come back. For one thing, I'd really, really like to meet the guy. I've never seen anything like it—outside the movies, anyway."

She sat up in the bed, her shadow tall beside him. "What guy? What are you talking about?"

He raised himself on one elbow. "Don't tell me you missed it. The one-man cavalry charge?"

She went very still. "You mean…you saw him, too?" Her breath left her in a rush. "I thought I imagined him. I thought—being in shock and all—I thought I'd conjured him from all those old movies I saw when I was little. That, and the old man I saw at the creek—I thought it was him, you know, mixed up somehow with John Wayne." There was a rustling as she settled back into the curve of his body. "I guess it really was him—the old man, I mean, not John Wayne. I wonder who he is. I'll have to ask Josie—I'm sure she must know. We need to thank him for saving our lives."

"You mean…you really don't know?" J.J.'s voice was hushed with wonder. "You *still* haven't met him?"

"Know…what? Met who?"

He laughed and kissed the top of her head. "Sweetheart, I don't know how to break this to you, but that old man, the one who saved your life and probably mine and Sage's as well—that was your grandpa, darlin'. Sierra Sam Malone."

Epilogue

From the memoirs of Sierra Sam Malone:

Ah, Elizabeth. I was too young and stupid to know it then, but you were the real thing...the treasure I had in my hands, that I threw away to go chasing after Fool's Gold.

In my defense, I will say that she was beautiful, more beautiful than anything I'd ever seen. As beautiful, I thought then, as an angel.

Elizabeth, you were the earth, the world, practical and real and as vital as food and drink to me. But...they say a man can't live on bread alone, and she...well, she was the food of my spirit. My soul. Her name was Barbara Chase, and I flew to her, and for a time, God help me, I did believe I'd found heaven.

* * * * *

Harlequin

ROMANTIC
SUSPENSE

COMING NEXT MONTH

Available May 31, 2011

#1659 ENEMY WATERS
Justine Davis

#1660 STRANGERS WHEN WE MEET
Code Name: Danger
Merline Lovelace

#1661 DESERT KNIGHTS
Bodyguard Sheik by Linda Conrad
Sheik's Captive by Loreth Anne White

#1662 THE CEO'S SECRET BABY
Karen Whiddon

You can find more information on upcoming
Harlequin® titles, free excerpts and more at
www.HarlequinInsideRomance.com.

REQUEST YOUR FREE BOOKS!
2 FREE NOVELS PLUS 2 FREE GIFTS!

ROMANTIC
SUSPENSE
Sparked by Danger, Fueled by Passion.

YES! Please send me 2 FREE Harlequin® Romantic Suspense novels and my 2 FREE gifts (gifts are worth about $10). After receiving them, if I don't wish to receive any more books, I can return the shipping statement marked "cancel." If I don't cancel, I will receive 4 brand-new novels every month and be billed just $4.24 per book in the U.S. or $4.99 per book in Canada. That's a saving of at least 15% off the cover price! It's quite a bargain! Shipping and handling is just 50¢ per book in the U.S. and 75¢ per book in Canada.* I understand that accepting the 2 free books and gifts places me under no obligation to buy anything. I can always return a shipment and cancel at any time. Even if I never buy another book, the two free books and gifts are mine to keep forever.

240/340 SDN FC95

Name _____ (PLEASE PRINT) _____

Address _____ Apt. #

City _____ State/Prov. _____ Zip/Postal Code

Signature (if under 18, a parent or guardian must sign)

Mail to the **Reader Service:**
IN U.S.A.: P.O. Box 1867, Buffalo, NY 14240-1867
IN CANADA: P.O. Box 609, Fort Erie, Ontario L2A 5X3

Not valid for current subscribers to Harlequin Romantic Suspense books.

Want to try two free books from another line?
Call 1-800-873-8635 or visit www.ReaderService.com.

* Terms and prices subject to change without notice. Prices do not include applicable taxes. Sales tax applicable in N.Y. Canadian residents will be charged applicable taxes. Offer not valid in Quebec. This offer is limited to one order per household. All orders subject to credit approval. Credit or debit balances in a customer's account(s) may be offset by any other outstanding balance owed by or to the customer. Please allow 4 to 6 weeks for delivery. Offer available while quantities last.

Your Privacy—The Reader Service is committed to protecting your privacy. Our Privacy Policy is available online at www.ReaderService.com or upon request from the Reader Service.

We make a portion of our mailing list available to reputable third parties that offer products we believe may interest you. If you prefer that we not exchange your name with third parties, or if you wish to clarify or modify your communication preferences, please visit us at www.ReaderService.com/consumerschoice or write to us at Reader Service Preference Service, P.O. Box 9062, Buffalo, NY 14269. Include your complete name and address.

HRS11

Harlequin® Blaze™ brings you
New York Times *and* USA TODAY *bestselling author*
Vicki Lewis Thompson with three new steamy titles
from the bestselling miniseries SONS OF CHANCE

Chance isn't just the last name of these rugged
Wyoming cowboys—it's their motto, too!

Read on for a sneak peek at the first title,
SHOULD'VE BEEN A COWBOY

Available June 2011 only from Harlequin® Blaze™.

"THANKS FOR NOT TURNING ON THE LIGHTS," Tyler said. "I'm a mess."

"Not in my book." Even in low light, Alex had a good view of her yellow shirt plastered to her body. It was all he could do not to reach for her, mud and all. But the next move needed to be hers, not his.

She slicked her wet hair back and squeezed some water out of the ends as she glanced upward. "I like the sound of the rain on a tin roof."

"Me, too."

She met his gaze briefly and looked away. "Where's the sink?"

"At the far end, beyond the last stall."

Tyler's running shoes squished as she walked down the aisle between the rows of stalls. She glanced sideways at Alex. "So how much of a cowboy are you these days? Do you ride the range and stuff?"

"I ride." He liked being able to say that. "Why?"

"Just wondered. Last summer, you were still a city boy. You even told me you weren't the cowboy type, but you're…different now."

He wasn't sure if that was a good thing or a bad thing. Maybe she preferred city boys to cowboys. "How am I different?"

"Well, you dress differently, and your hair's a little longer. Your face seems a little more chiseled, but maybe that's because of your hair. Also, there's something else, something harder to define, an attitude…"

"Are you saying I have an attitude?"

"Not in a bad way. It's more like a quiet confidence."

He was flattered, but still he had to laugh. "I just admitted a while ago that I have all kinds of doubts about this event tomorrow. That doesn't seem like quiet confidence to me."

"This isn't about your job, it's about…your…" She took a deep breath. "It's about your sex appeal, okay? I have no business talking about it, because it will only make me want to do things I shouldn't do." She started toward the end of the barn. "Now, where's that sink? We need to get cleaned up and go back to the house. Dinner is probably ready, and I—"

He spun her around and pulled her into his arms, mud and all. "Let's do those things." Then he kissed her, knowing that she would kiss him back, knowing that this time he would take that kiss where he wanted it to go. And she would let him.

Follow Tyler and Alex's wild adventures in
SHOULD'VE BEEN A COWBOY
Available June 2011 only from Harlequin® Blaze™
wherever books are sold.

Harlequin

SPECIAL EDITION

Life, Love and Family

LOVE CAN BE FOUND IN THE MOST UNLIKELY PLACES, ESPECIALLY WHEN YOU'RE NOT LOOKING FOR IT...

Failed marriages, broken families and disappointment. Cecilia and Brandon have both been unlucky in love and life and are ripe for an intervention. Good thing Brandon's mother happens to stumble upon this matchmaking project. But will Brandon be able to open his eyes and get away from his busy career to see that all he needs is right there in front of him?

FIND OUT IN

WHAT THE SINGLE DAD WANTS...

BY *USA TODAY* BESTSELLING AUTHOR

MARIE FERRARELLA

AVAILABLE IN JUNE 2011
WHEREVER BOOKS ARE SOLD.

www.eHarlequin.com

SE0611MF